W9-BZW-464

DISCARD

THE HEAT IS ON

NEXT BEST JUNIOR CHEF

EPISODE 2

THE HEAT IS ON

by **Charise Mericle Harper**

with illustrations by **Aurélie Blard-Quintard**

HOUGHTON MIFFLIN HARCOURT
Boston   New York

The text was set in Garamond Premier Pro.

Library of Congress Cataloging-in-Publication Data
Names: Harper, Charise Mericle, author. | Blard-Quintard, Aurélie,
illustrator.
Title: The heat is on / by Charise Mericle Harper ; with illustrations by
Aurélie Blard-Quintard.
Description: Boston ; New York : Houghton Mifflin Harcourt, [2018]. | Series:
Next Best Junior Chef ; episode 2 | Summary: The second week of Next Best
Junior Chef features family and traditions, as Caroline, Oliver, and Rae,
ages eleven to twelve, face more challenges and another elimination.
Identifiers: LCCN 2017004283 | ISBN 9780544980280 (paper over board)
Subjects: | CYAC: Cooking—Fiction. | Contests—Fiction. |
Television—Production and direction—Fiction. | Friendship—Fiction. |
BISAC: JUVENILE FICTION / Cooking & Food. | JUVENILE FICTION / Action &
Adventure / General. | JUVENILE FICTION / Humorous Stories. | JUVENILE
FICTION / Performing Arts / Television & Radio. | JUVENILE FICTION / Media
Tie-In. | JUVENILE FICTION / Business, Careers, Occupations.
Classification: LCC PZ7.H231323 Hc 2017 | DDC [Fic]—dc23
LC record available at https://lccn.loc.gov/2017004283

Manufactured in the United States of America
DOC 10 9 8 7 6 5 4 3 2 1
4500692892

For the home cooks,
and the powerful memories folded,
stirred, and shaped by their food.

CHAPTER 1

Caroline, Oliver, and Rae were lined up outside the studio door, the same as a week ago with two exceptions: Tate was missing and they were excited instead of nervous. Tate had been sent home at the end of last week's episode, but the biggest change was the excitement—after a week of competing, they had more of an idea of what to expect. In just minutes, the announcer would call their names and they'd be walking down the ramp to greet the judges.

Caroline spun around and whispered a fast "Good luck."

Oliver frowned. "I don't need luck."

Rae returned a thumbs-up. "You too."

"Shhh!" Chef Nancy held a finger to her lips.

Caroline flushed, faced front, and a second later . . .

"BOOMS!"

"LIGHTS!"

"CAMERAS!"

"ROLLING!"

... it started.

The announcer's voice filled the room. "Welcome to *Next Best Junior Chef*! This is week two of our competition and things are about to get *hot* in the kitchen. We're down to three junior chefs. They're the best in the nation, but can they handle the challenges we've cooked up? Will the King of Calm keep his cool? Are the bonds of friendship about to be sliced and diced? Thursday's elimination round will leave us with the final two contestants. One of these talented chefs *will be* the Next Best Junior Chef! Let's bring out our three young contestants."

Chef Nancy tapped Caroline's shoulder—it was the signal to walk through the door. Caroline stepped forward and smiled all the way to the front of the studio.

The announcer continued. "Congratulations, Caroline, and welcome to week two. Caroline is eleven years old and from Chicago, Illinois. She's got some tricks up her sleeve. Not everyone can turn an eggplant into a delectable dessert. The judges have been continuously impressed with her skill and creativity."

Oliver's foot hit the ramp just as the announcer said his name. He marched forward, head up, and with only a hint of a smirk. This was serious. He wasn't here for fun.

"Congratulations, Oliver, and welcome to another exciting week. Oliver is twelve years old and from Montgomery, Alabama. He's our reigning champ from last week, and this will give him an edge in today's competition. Last week we saw this King of Calm step up and save the day. The judges all agree: This junior chef is some kind of superhero in the kitchen, too."

Chef Nancy tapped Rae's shoulder and then gave it a squeeze.

Rae grinned and moved out into the bright lights. She wasn't worried about fainting again—that was a last-week thing, she was sure of it.

"Congratulations, Rae, and welcome back to the competition. Rae is eleven years old and from Port Chester, New

York. She got off to a bit of a rocky start last week, but that hasn't slowed her down. She's feisty, determined, and a master of culinary presentation. The judges have not been disappointed. This young chef knows how to wow both the eye and the palate."

Rae moved in next to Oliver and faced the judges.

"Our esteemed judges include Chef Vera Porter of the famous Porter Farm Restaurant, the renowned pastry chef Aimee Copley, and Chef Gary Lee, restaurant proprietor and host of the award-winning show *Adventures in Cooking*. The judges will be watching our competitors very closely throughout the week, and everything that happens along the way *will* be taken into consideration when we get to the final elimination round In addition to choosing a winner, the judges will have to dismiss one of our junior chefs and ask them to hang up their apron. This decision will be based on performance,

the taste and presentation of their dishes, and overall creative vision.

"Our junior chefs are mentored by Chef Nancy Patel, the 2013 recipient of the Golden Spoon Award.

"The winner of *Next Best Junior Chef* will receive two life-changing prizes: a custom food truck *and* a guest spot on *Adventures in Cooking* when it begins filming this summer in Italy!"

Chef Gary stepped forward, his arms opened wide. "Welcome, young chefs! Are we all excited to be back?"

"YES, CHEF!"

He rubbed his hands. "Are you ready for the surprises? The unexpected? The twists and turns?"

"Yes, Chef!"

"Hmm." Chef Gary studied the contestants and stroked his chin. "Not so enthusiastic that time. Well, you're probably right to be worried. This is not going to be easy. It will be challenging and—"

"FUN!" interrupted Chef Aimee. "We're going to have fun." She winked at Caroline. "I promise!"

Caroline breathed a sigh of relief. Chef Gary's joking around was making her nervous. The wink helped a lot.

Rae glanced down the line of judges. Chef Porter was wearing her sour-pickle face. A minute later it disappeared.

Chef Porter cleared her throat and smiled. "The focus for this week is sharing, here, with us and with others. We want to learn about your families, your traditions, and your inspirations, because these are the things that shape creativity. It's going to be an exciting and fulfilling week!"

"CUT!" Steve the producer waved his arms and the cameras turned off.

Chef Gary and Chef Aimee stepped around the table to shake everyone's hand and wish them luck, but not Chef Porter. She was already gone.

After the greetings, Chef Nancy pointed to the orange door on the far wall. "Interview time, and it's the same format as last week. When Steve asks a question, just answer honestly."

"Me first," said Oliver. He pushed to the front and marched across the room. A minute later he was sitting on the stool facing Steve the producer and Mark the cameraman.

"Ready?" asked Steve.

Oliver nodded.

Steve signaled the camera. "Tell me, Oliver, do you have a pet?"

OLIVER

I have a cat. His name is Muscadine. That's a kind of grape that grows in Alabama. But we don't call him that anymore, because Muscadine is hard to say, especially if you have to shout it out loud a lot. Cats aren't good listeners. We just call him Deeno.

I have a pet goldfish. He's five years old, which is pretty old for a goldfish. My mom wanted to call him a French name like Celeste, but my dad promised me that I could pick the name. It's not easy to tell if a goldfish is a boy or a girl. Stanley doesn't care: as long as I feed him, he's happy.

CAROLINE

RAE

I don't really have a pet. There are two white ducks down at the pond a block from my house, and sometimes when we have old bread I'll go down there and feed them. They're really tame—some people even touch and pet them, but I'm not really a close-up duck person. I just like watching from the distance.

CHAPTER 2

Lunch was set out on the big round table at Porter Lodge. Rae looked out the window at the large grassy field and the wooded forest in the distance. This was definitely the nicest place she'd ever stayed. The lodge was huge, and everything inside was top-notch fancy. She grabbed a mini sandwich and slouched back in her chair, resting her knees against the table. It wasn't home, but after a week, she was used to it. She waited for Caroline and Oliver to pick a seat. No one sat in Tate's spot. She shuffled to a new position so she wouldn't have to look at the empty chair. She'd miss his jokes.

Chef Nancy rushed through the room with a stack of papers. "I'll be back in five minutes. Start eating. We have a busy afternoon."

Rae nibbled the crust of her sandwich. "Why don't people like the crust? It's my favorite part."

"It's the bread," answered Oliver. "Good bread means good crust." He bit into his sandwich.

"And the filling," added Caroline. "That's important too. You have to spread it right to the edge of the crust or all you'll get is a mouth full of dry bread."

Rae pointed her sandwich at Caroline. "Thanks for the tip, but I'm pretty sure we won't be making sandwiches this week."

Oliver was still chewing, but he nodded in agreement.

Rae caught Caroline staring at Tate's chair. She lowered her lip. "I miss him too."

They both looked at Oliver. He shrugged and changed the subject. "Did they ask you a pet question in your interview?"

Caroline brightened. "Yeah, I have a goldfish and—"

Oliver's raised his hand. "Stop." He leaned forward and lowered his voice. "That's a clue. I'll bet you anything, the next challenge has something to do with pets."

Rae scanned the room. She motioned for the others to crowd closer. "This is exactly what we should be doing. Working together! Helping each other. What if we made a pact? A stick-together pact!" She studied Oliver. "We agree to stick together, share information, and help, that way we can all do our best."

"And focus our energy on cooking!" Caroline threw her hands in the air. "I'M IN! Stick-together pact! STP!"

Rae raised her arm. "In!"

Oliver tapped his finger on the table, studied it, then

looked up and pointed. "Okay, but this is a still a competition. I'm going to do everything I can to win."

Caroline grinned eagerly. "Of course! We all are, and . . . may the best chef win!"

••••

When Chef Nancy returned to the room, everyone was talking and joking. She smiled. This was the kind of energy she'd been hoping for since day one.

She moved to the head of the table. "Just a few things before we get started. We will not be using camera cards this week. Last week we used them so you'd learn to be more comfortable in front of the cameras. This week I assume you are all sufficiently trained and know the rules." Her eyes settled on Oliver. He'd learned the hard way—losing last week had stung. This week he would not hog the camera.

She continued. "Great! Let's head to the school studio. I want to introduce some new features in this week's competition."

••••

The school studio had not changed: the workstations were clean and ready to be used, and the Gadget Wall was still at the far end of the room, festooned with shiny kitchen tools.

Chef Nancy gathered the group around the table at the front and pulled out a large black board with three names across the top. "Every time you win a regular challenge or a mini-challenge, I will put a star under your name. On

Wednesday evening, the contestant with the most stars will be named the winner of . . ." She reached under the table and pulled out a shiny gold envelope. It sparkled and shimmered under the studio lights.

"The Golden Envelope!"

Rae gasped, Oliver clenched his fists, and Caroline felt a shiver run down her spine. They all wanted it.

Chef Nancy continued. "It will be opened on Thursday morning to reveal a special advantage for the winner, to be used in this week's elimination challenge."

It was hard to concentrate on anything else, but Chef Nancy was already moving on. She handed out the schedule for the week. "As you can see we're fired up and ready to get things started. We'll move into our first challenge right after this meeting. The judges will be more involved this week— and that's a compliment. They really want to learn about your inspirations and process." Chef Nancy tapped the schedule. "I'll give you a few minutes to go over this."

Caroline studied the paper. "Eight challenges! How many did we have last week?"

"Fewer," answered Rae. "Six including the elimination challenge."

NEXT BEST JUNIOR CHEF

CONFIDENTIAL!
Schedule of Events for
Week Two (Episode Two)

Friday
  Challenge
Saturday
  Lesson
  Mini-challenge
Sunday
  Challenge
Monday
  Field trip!
  Challenge
  Lesson

Tuesday
  Challenge
Wednesday
  Field trip!
  Mini-challenge
  Mini-challenge
Thursday
  Elimination challenge

Oliver waved his hand in the air. "Excuse me, ma'am. Will I get to use my advantage today? The one from last week? Remember? I picked fire."

Chef Nancy shook her head. "Sorry, Oliver, no advance information."

Rae shot Caroline a look. Water and air—those were the leftover choices after fire. What did it mean? Was that good or bad? And how were they part of the challenge?

Chef Nancy started toward the door. Rae sighed and followed. It wouldn't be a long wait to find out. The challenge was next.

CHAPTER 3

Chef Nancy led everyone outside to the back of the lodge. She stopped at a small fenced-off grassy area in front of an impressive tent, with two large double doors, and big windows.

Oliver pointed to the door. "Do you know what's in there?" He didn't wait for an answer. "Our challenge."

Chef Nancy opened the gate and led the group onto the grass. "Wait here. I'm going inside, but I'll be right back." A minute later she emerged with Steve the producer and the camerapeople.

"ROLLING!" shouted Steve, and Chef Gary burst out the doors.

He jogged over to the group. "Phew! We had a little pet trouble, but now we're all good. Should we start?"

"YES, CHEF!"

Rae shot Caroline a look. Pet! Oliver *was* right!

Chef Gary grinned. "I know you're all pet lovers, so I

can't wait for you to meet *my* new pet. In just a minute Chef Aimee is going to—"

"EEEH!" Rae squealed.

Caroline hopped up and down and pointed.

Chef Gary turned. Chef Aimee was walking toward them holding a squirming puppy. He shook his head. "Well, upstaged again, but I don't mind. I love this little gal.

Chef Gary rubbed the dog's ears. "What a beauty. She's a long-haired dachshund."

Chef Aimee kneeled down. "Would you like to meet her? If you sit on the grass, I'll let her go."

Caroline, Rae, and Oliver dropped to the ground. A minute later they were in puppy heaven.

Rae stroked her ears. "They're so soft!"

"I want to hug her forever!" said Caroline. The puppy wriggled out of her arms and headed straight for Oliver.

"Fiesty!" Oliver tried to raise his arm, but the puppy was tugging on his shirt sleeve.

"Oh, dear! Sorry, Oliver." Chef Aimee pried the puppy away. "I guess she needs some training."

"That's okay, ma'am. I have lots of shirts."

"What's her name?" asked Caroline.

"Good question!" answered Chef Gary. "We haven't decided. Any suggestions?"

The puppy raced circles around them. Happy to be free.

"How about Turbo?" suggested Oliver. "She's pretty fast."

Chef Gary nodded. "Good idea. You know, the dachshund was bred to chase and catch small animals."

"Freckles!" shouted Caroline. "Because she has three little spots right on her chin."

"Good observation!" said Chef Aimee. She scooped the puppy up and looked at Rae. "What about you, Rae? Any ideas?"

Rae looked around nervously. Something about this was a trick. The cameras, the puppy, the name . . . hadn't the others noticed? Maybe this was a chance to get ahead. She had to be smart. What kind of name would a chef like? "Umami!"

"Oh!" Chef Aimee stepped back and handed the puppy to Chef Nancy. "Interesting. Can you explain?"

"Well, umami is a special taste sensation, and this puppy is obviously special—plus you can call her . . . Uma for short." Rae grinned.

Caroline and Oliver both frowned.

Chef Gary pointed to the puppy. "This kind of dog is sometimes called a hot dog, because of its long body and short legs. So, let's introduce our first challenge." He motioned for everyone to stand. "We're calling it the Diner Challenge! And today's menu special is . . . HOT DOGS!"

Caroline gasped. Hot dogs for a cooking challenge? Rae and Oliver looked surprised too.

Chef Gary continued. "For this challenge, we are asking you to create a hot dog with toppings that are representational of the name you suggested for our puppy. In addition to the hot dog, you'll also be making a potato accompaniment. No french fries or potato chips—we want to see ingenuity in your side dish."

Chef Aimee held up three cards. "Oliver, will you please step forward? When you won the last challenge your advantage was a choice of fire, water, or air. Which did you choose?"

Oliver smirked. "I picked fire, ma'am."

Chef Aimee looked through the cards and handed one

to Oliver. She waved the two remaining cards. "One of these is water and the other is air. Oliver, will you please pass these out to the remaining contestants—one card to each."

Oliver studied the cards, then handed them out.

"Assignments received! Now let's have some fun."

"CUT!" yelled Steve.

The cameras turned off and Chef Nancy rushed forward. She was still holding the dog, but she waved her one free hand. "Quick, into the tent."

Rae stepped next to Caroline and held out her card. "Water! What do you think it means?"

Caroline shook her head. "I don't know, but I bet Oliver does. He's smiling."

CHAPTER 4

The interior of the tent was set up exactly like the filming studio, with workstations, a table at the front, a pantry, and the Gadget Wall. Chef Nancy lined everyone up behind the big table.

Chef Gary and Chef Aimee stood on the other side, waiting. The puppy was nowhere in sight.

"ROLLING!" shouted Steve, and the cameras turned on.

Chef Gary smiled. It was his sneaky smile. Rae was instantly worried.

"There is of course a twist in this challenge, and that twist is determined by the card in your hand. Oliver, you have fire—that means you may only use the stovetop flames and direct heat to prepare your hot dog and side dish."

Chef Gary turned to Caroline. "Caroline, you hold the air card. That means you may only use hot air to prepare your hot dog and side dish."

NEXT BEST JUNIOR CHEF

Rae looked around nervously. Wait! She had water! WA-TER! How could you be creative with water?

Chef Gary smiled at Rae. "And finally the water card. Rae, that means you may only cook with water to prepare your hot dog and side dish."

Chef Gary raised his hand. "You have sixty minutes for this challenge, and we want to see some real out of the box thinking. The pantry will be open for the duration of this challenge."

Rae glared at her card. Water was impossible. Oliver gave her the worst card on purpose!

Chef Gary clasped his hands. "Okay! Before we get to work, let's talk about the prize. The winner of this challenge will be featured in a photo spread with their recipe in *Creative Cooking*. As you know, *Creative Cooking* is one of the most distinguished culinary magazines published today."

Caroline and Oliver both smiled.

"And each week, the junior chefs get to have fun outside the kitchen with Chef Gary." Chef Aimee nudged Chef Gary. "The winner of this challenge will get to decide his fate!"

Now Rae smiled too. Last week had been fun. She'd knocked Chef Gary right off his seat into the green Jell-O dunk tank.

Chef Gary pointed to the clock. "To your workstations. The clock is about to start. Are we excited?"

"YES, CHEF!"

"Ready?"

"YES, CHEF."

"CUT!" yelled Steve.

The cameras turned off.

Chef Nancy stepped forward. "This is a hard one, so we're going to give you a little extra time. Instead of five minutes to plan, you'll actually have twenty minutes and I'll come around to help."

When the show was on TV, no one would know about the twenty minutes. It was just how the show worked. None of the junior chefs complained. Extra time was always a good thing.

RAE

Oliver gave me water. Why? It's for sure the hardest challenge. My hot dog is called the Umami Dog, so it has to be extra delicious, because of the name and, well, because I want to win. No, I haven't even thought about the potato side dish. Ha! Who has time to think about it? I guess I'll just boil them.

Chef Nancy walked straight to Rae's workstation. "How is it going?"

"Boil!" complained Rae. "How can I make something amazing if I don't get to fry, or bake, or broil, or sauté, or glaze, or anything?" She slumped over the counter.

Chef Nancy patted her shoulder. "You've been given an opportunity. You can wow the judges. Turn it around. Think about what you *can* use. Tap in to your creative spirit."

Rae nodded. Chef Nancy was right—she needed to change her thinking. Step one: How was she going to give her hot dog the umami flavor?

This is a competition. I had to give the water card to *someone*. I think Rae has the skills to handle it. She might not win, but she'll be okay. She won't freeze up and fall apart. I'm excited about my Turbo Dog. My hot dog has the best name. If you saw it on a menu, you'd order it. Potatoes on the stove? Not hard at all. I already have a bunch of ideas.

OLIVER

Oliver was busy writing a pantry list when Chef Nancy approached. "So, Oliver, are you comfortable with this challenge? Any questions?"

He didn't look up. "No questions, ma'am. I'm going to make a spicy sriracha sauce, homemade ketchup, and a potato rosti." He added a few items to his list.

Chef Nancy tapped the table. "Remember, Oliver: the judges have asked to see creativity. In this instance simple will not be best."

Oliver looked up. "Thank you, ma'am. I'll remember

that." He scratched something off his list. Chef Nancy was right. He needed to exceed expectations. His potatoes had to be amazing.

CAROLINE

I'm glad I got the air card. Poor Rae —water is pretty much impossible. All she can do is boil. I hope she can make it work. I already know what the freckle part of my Freckle Dog will be—pickled jalapeños. I'll use three, one for each spot on the puppy. I haven't decided on the potatoes yet, but I have the oven, so it won't be hard to make something that'll impress the judges.

Caroline couldn't wait to tell Chef Nancy about her plans. "The hot dog will be sweet and spicy just like the puppy, because she has some feistiness in her. But I'm especially excited about the potatoes. I'm making stuffed potato cups and I'll use mini muffin tins to shape them."

Chef Nancy nodded. "Be sure to get them into the oven as soon as possible. Sixty minutes will go by faster than you think."

Before she moved off to the side, Chef Nancy offered some last words of advice to the group. "If you make a mistake, ask yourself, *How can I solve this problem?* There's no time for worrying. Innovate!"

CHAPTER 5

"PLACES, EVERYONE!" Steve held up his hand. "And cameras . . . rolling!"

Chef Gary stood at the front of the room. "You'll have five minutes in the pantry and then we'll start cooking, but remember, if you've forgotten anything you *can* go back. Get ready. Your time starts . . . NOW!"

Caroline, Oliver, and Rae grabbed their baskets and raced into the pantry. Rae recited the five ingredients from the top of her list: "Anchovy paste, soy sauce, tomato paste, fish sauce, and olive oil." No one cared that she talked to herself—they were used to it. Ten minutes ago she'd been desperate, but now she was on a mission. "Umami paste to the rescue!"

"TIME!" shouted Chef Aimee.

Everyone raced back to their workstations.

A minute later, Chef Aimee gave the official start. "LET'S GET COOKING!"

The camerapeople moved in for a close-up of Oliver's workstation. His first step was *mise en place*—that was French for "everything in its place." Everything needed to be chopped, measured, and portioned into bowls before he even started cooking. The benefits were huge—less chance of making a mistake, and faster access to the ingredients.

Caroline grabbed her potatoes and started peeling. There was a lot to do.

Chef Aimee came by just as she began grating. "Oh dear, are you okay?"

Tears steamed down Caroline's face. She nodded. "It's the onions, but I'm almost done." She dumped the grated potatoes and onions in a dishtowel and moved over to the sink. "I need to wring these out and get them as dry as possible, because extra moisture will make my potato cups soggy."

"Clever," said Chef Aimee. "I'm impressed."

Caroline blushed.

I'm cooking my hot dog in the oven. I don't want it to dry out, so I'll put it in a baking dish with just a little beef consommé and roast it at around 400 degrees for ten to twelve minutes. The consommé will help it stay moist, and the baking will make it perfectly brown.

CAROLINE

Rae was waiting for Chef Aimee when she arrived. She held up a mason jar. "Pickled onions. I made them right away, so the onions would have time to absorb the flavor of the vinegar." She dipped a spoon into her bowl and stirred. "And now I'm making an umami paste."

Chef Aimee leaned over to look. "What's in it?"

Rae rattled off a list of ingredients, and then stopped. "Oh no! I forgot the Parmesan cheese."

Chef Aimee pointed to the pantry. "Well, don't waste time talking to me."

Rae gave a fast wave and ran off. When she came back

Chef Aimee was gone. Too bad—she'd wanted to tell her about her potato salad. Hopefully no one else was using sweet potatoes. Rae grabbed the Parmesan cheese and quickly grated it into the bowl. The potatoes were next, and if they weren't peeled and boiling in the next five minutes she'd be in trouble. She sighed. This was definitely going to be a race, up until the very last minute.

RAE

I'm going to boil my hot dog, but not just in water. I'll add salt, vinegar, cumin, and nutmeg. After five minutes in a simmering bath, it'll be perfect.

Oliver was Chef Aimee's last stop. His countertop was filled with bowls, tools, cutting boards, pots, pans, and Oliver was racing back and forth.

Chef Aimee watched, shaking her head. "Oliver, what's going on here? This isn't how you usually work. It looks . . . kind of crazy."

Oliver nodded. "Yes, ma'am. I know, but there's so much to do."

Chef Aimee put her hand on his shoulder. "Let's take a breather, just for a minute. Take me through your process."

Oliver pointed to each bowl and identified it. "Bowl one is sriracha barbecue sauce—still needs paprika and Worcestershire sauce. Bowl two: sauce to add to the red onion marmalade once the onions are done cooking. Bowl three: homemade ketchup—I'll add this finishing sauce once I've blended the tomatoes, onions, vinegar, water, and sugar in the food processor." Oliver fidgeted and pointed to a stack of potatoes. "I'm sorry, ma'am. I really need to get to those if I'm going to finish my rosti on time."

Chef Aimee raised her arms and stepped back. "Of course, Oliver, continue. I don't know how you did it, but it looks like you've got this under control."

OLIVER

> I've scored my hot dog and am marinating it in a mixture of oil, homemade ketchup, soy sauce, and garlic. It'll absorb these flavors and the moisture from the sauce. When I put it in the pan, it will steam on the inside and grill on the outside. It's the best way to make a perfectly cooked hot dog. And I'll use bacon fat instead of butter.

••••

"Thirty minutes," called Chef Gary.

"No!" Caroline banged a spatula on the table.

Chef Gary rushed over to check on her.

"Ugh!" She dropped the spatula and picked up a fork. The mini potato cups were sticking to the muffin tin.

Chef Gary stepped up and sniffed. "Mmm, smells good. Might be worth the trouble to get them out."

Caroline smiled halfheartedly and attacked the tin again. This time the plump potato cup popped right out. She picked up a bowl and started mixing.

Chef Gary watched. "What's that?"

"Homemade ranch dressing."

He covered his mouth. "I'd better go before I start drooling."

"Eye on the clock! FIFTEEN MINUTES!" Chef Aimee clapped her hands.

That was just enough time for the last two visits—Rae and Oliver.

Chef Gary picked a skewer off Rae's table and twirled it. "I think we've seen these recently."

"Yes, Chef, but with a new recipe. I'm making potato salad on a stick . . . with sweet potatoes." She dropped a quarter cup of diced poblano chiles into her bowl of potato chunks. "I have to mix these in carefully—I don't want to smash my potatoes." She picked up a wooden spoon and carefully folded the ingredients together.

Chef Gary returned the skewer. "Good work, Rae! I can't wait to try that flavor combination."

"Sweet and spicy to go with umami!" Rae looked up to smile at Chef Gary, but he was already heading off to see Oliver.

Oliver was shaking his head and his frying pan.
"What's cooking?" asked Chef Gary.

"Not this potato rosti!" snapped Oliver. Then he quickly apologized. "I'm sorry, sir, but it's these potatoes. I want crispy, not soggy."

"Creative problem-solving." Chef Gary tapped his head. "Take a minute and think it through."

Did Oliver have a minute? When Chef Gary yelled "hands up," he'd have to drop everything—ready or not.

He took a deep breath, and studied his pan. Suddenly, he knew what to do. "Thank you, Chef!" His pan was too crowded. The rosti was steaming not frying. He sliced the rosti into eighths and pulled out four pie-shaped wedges. A minute later, four remaining slices were back on the stove, crisping up.

Chef Gary walked to the center of the room. "FIVE MINUTES!"

"AHHH!" Rae drizzled five droplets of poblano honey dressing on the side of the plate.

Oliver cut three thin wedges of potato rosti and balanced them on edge next to a small ramekin of ketchup.

Caroline stacked three mini potato cups one on top of another and was just about to add a few chopped scallions when . . .

"TIME! HANDS UP!" called Chef Gary.

"CUT!" yelled Steve.

CHAPTER 6

The camera crew followed Steve to each workstation to get close-ups of the food. Caroline, Rae, and Oliver stood to the side, watching.

CAROLINE: I can't wait for the judges to try my potato cups, because there's a surprise inside—a tangy ranch sauce filling. I don't think anyone is going to miss the chopped scallions.

Five minutes later everyone was back in position for judging.

"AND ROLLING!" shouted Steve.

Chef Gary pointed to Rae. "Rae, will you please bring your dish to the table?"

She looked around nervously, then lifted her plate and started toward the front. It was a surprise to be first.

I know the judges are going to like my hot dog. The umami sauce is rich and complex, and it goes perfectly with the tangy pickled onions.

RAE

Chef Gary studied her plate. "I see you're using skewers, but I would have never thought to bend them into triangles. Clever! It's a creative presentation."

"Thank you, Chef." Rae clamped her hands tightly together behind her back. No one needed to know they were shaking.

"What have you made for us?" asked Chef Aimee.

"I have an Umami Dog with pickled onions, accompanied by a sweet potato salad with a poblano honey dressing."

Chef Gary cut the hot dog into three pieces.

Rae held her breath while the judges took bites.

"Wow! Complex but satisfying," said Chef Gary.

Chef Nancy licked her lips. "That sauce is delicious. I could eat it with a spoon."

Chef Aimee shook her head. "I want what you had, but my end of the hot dog is just bun and wiener. Where's the umami sauce?"

Rae covered her mouth, horrified. Caroline's words

flashed through her mind: *You have to spread the filling right to the edge of the crust.* What a mistake!

Chef Gary broke the skewer into three—one piece for each of them.

"Oh my gosh!" Chef Aimee covered her mouth. "This is good!"

Chef Nancy nodded. "Like a firework in my mouth! There's the pow of spice and then the satisfying sweetness of the potato."

Chef Gary dipped his potato back into the sauce on the plate.

"Double dipper!" teased Chef Aimee. "But I don't blame you." She reached in and did the same.

"Impressive! All of it!" said Chef Gary.

"Thank you, chefs." Rae quickly walked back to her workstation. Disappointing a judge was not a good feeling, but there'd been more good than bad. Maybe she still had a chance.

My hot dog and my rosti are bursting with flavor. When the name is Turbo, you have to deliver a big experience. The judges are definitely going to want more than just one bite.

OLIVER

Oliver walked confidently over to the table. This was his to win. Rae's mistake had cost her points, and Caroline wasn't much of a threat.

Chef Aimee studied Oliver's plate. "Oliver, I like your presentation. It's interesting to see a balancing act on the plate. Can you tell us what you've made?"

"Yes, ma'am. This is a Turbo Dog with a sriracha barbecue sauce and an onion-bacon relish. And balanced on the edge here are three slices of my bacon and scallion potato rosti." Oliver pointed to the ramekin. "And tangy homemade ketchup."

Chef Aimee dipped a crispy potato slice into the ketchup. "Mmm, bacon-y!"

Chef Gary pretended to push her aside. "Let me at it. I love bacon!"

He took a bite and closed his eyes. "I hope there's more of this left in the pan. I'll eat it for lunch."

Chef Nancy agreed. "I'll help you."

Chef Gary shook his head. "Nope, all mine!"

Everyone laughed.

"And now for the Turbo Dog." Chef Gary divided the hot dog.

Chef Aimee took the biggest piece. "That's a great name, very catchy."

They each took a bite.

"Nice spice," said Chef Aimee.

"Bacon-y!" said Chef Gary.

"Um, very," added Chef Nancy.

Oliver couldn't help but smile. He was winning.

"Too much?" asked Chef Gary.

Chef Nancy and Chef Aimee both nodded.

The smile faded.

Chef Gary moved his hand over the plate. "This whole thing . . . I hate to say it, but it's just one flavor. Bacon! I love bacon, but we're losing the taste of the hot dog and any other spices that might be in here. It might work if we called it the Bacon Dog, but even that might be a stretch. Am I right? Is there bacon in everything?"

Oliver paused. "Uh . . . yes, sir. I fried the hot dog in bacon fat and there's bacon in the relish and bacon in the potato rosti."

Chef Gary stepped back from the plate. "Unfortunately, more is not always better, but on their own, the rosti and the ketchup are delicious. Thank you, Oliver."

Oliver walked back to his station. Later he'd probably be embarrassed, but right now he was just numb.

Chef Aimee called Caroline to the table. "Caroline, what have you made us?"

Caroline pointed out the items on her plate. "It's a Freckles Dog with a peach vidalia onion salsa with three jalapeños—one for each freckle on the puppy. And my potato dish is baked onion Parmesan hash brown cups."

Chef Aimee leaned forward and took a hash brown

cup off the plate. One bite later she
was waving her hand up and down.
"There's something inside and it's . . .
delicious!"

Chef Gary agreed. "That's my kind
of surprise! And the tanginess of the
sauce is sophisticated." He eyed the
plate. "I could eat another."

Chef Nancy quickly snatched her piece away and bit into
it. "Wow! It's like a hash brown donut."

The Freckles dog was next. "Three pieces and one jala-
peño for each of us," announced Chef Gary. He popped his
piece into his mouth.

Chef Aimee examined the plate. "I like how it looks—
fresh and healthy—but hot dogs aren't very healthy, are they."
She laughed and took a bite. "Oh, wow! Yum!"

Chef Gary looked at Caroline and shook his head. "I'm
sad. You've given us a sample, but I want more! Your presentation is fresh and inviting and you really delivered on taste.
The sweet spicy combo is sophisticated, but not overpower-
ing. You let the hot dog shine through. Well done, Caroline."

Chef Nancy raised her hand. "I second that. I want more
too . . . with another potato donut, of course!"

"ME THREE!" added Chef Aimee, and everyone laughed.

Caroline walked slowly back to her workstation. This
was the singular best cooking review of her life, and she
wanted to remember every second of it.

The judges moved to the back of the room to discuss the challenge, but the winner wasn't going to be a surprise. Rae looked back and gave Caroline a thumbs-up and a big smile. A friend happy for a friend—Caroline was going to remember that, too.

CHAPTER 7

The judges called everyone to the front of the room.

"What a start," said Chef Gary. "It's like the three bears. Too much, too little, and just right. I think we all know who's our winning bear. Caroline, will you please step up? You are the winner of this challenge. We all loved the Freckles Dog, and the hash brown potato cups were ingenious. It's a recipe we're excited to share with the readers of *Creative Cooking.*"

Caroline blushed. "Thank you, Chef."

Chef Gary pointed to the Gadget Wall. "And it's time for a decision. You may pick a gadget from—"

"Not so fast!" Chef Aimee put her hand up. "There's plenty of time to pick out a gadget. Caroline has a bigger decision to make: the fate of Chef Gary!"

Chef Gary feigned surprise. "What? Are we doing that again?"

Chef Aimee turned to Oliver and Rae.

They nodded.

Chef Gary shrugged. "Really? Are you sure?"

"YES, CHEF!

Chef Aimee looked at Chef Gary. "An adventurous chef never says . . ."

"NO TO A CHALLENGE!" shouted the junior chefs.

Chef Gary threw his arms up. "Okay, you win! I'll do it."

Chef Aimee turned back to Caroline. "This week's fate of Chef Gary is Trick or Treat. Make your choice."

"Trick!" shouted Oliver.

"Trick!" yelled Rae.

Caroline looked back and forth between them. "Treat!"

Chef Nancy, off to the side where the cameras couldn't see her, made a clapping motion.

Rae and Oliver obeyed the cue and clapped, but it was halfhearted.

"CUT!" yelled Steve.

OLIVER

Caroline is acting weird. Maybe it's a power thing because she won. I don't know. She was supposed to pick Trick! Rae and I *both* told her to. If it's bad, it's not our fault.

Chef Nancy rushed forward and gathered the contestants together. "Caroline, you may go to the Gadget Wall and pick out your prize."

Caroline came back with a mortar and pestle.

"Good choice!" said Chef Nancy. "There's nothing like fresh-ground spices. We can put it in your toolbox later. Now out to the parking lot."

"Parking lot?" asked Caroline. "What kind of treat's in the parking lot?"

"A crummy one," complained Oliver. "But we're stuck with it."

Caroline scowled and grabbed Rae's arm. "You're wrong. I'm sure it'll be . . . amazing!" They followed Chef Nancy out the door, with Oliver grumbling behind them, then suddenly froze.

Oliver pushed to the front. "An obstacle course!"

"LOOK!" Rae pointed. "CHEF GARY is . . ." She burst out laughing.

Chef Gary was wearing roller skates and hanging on to Chef Aimee's shoulders like his life depended on it. She pulled him slowly towards them.

He shook his head. "This is a lot harder than it looks. I should have practiced."

Chef Aimee pointed to a table near the start of the course. It was filled with everything needed to make a fabulous sundae. "That's the ice cream station. You'll have two minutes to make a sundae, and then Chef Gary will pick them up, and head though the course of orange cones to the finish line. We're hoping he'll make it without falling down."

Rae leaned next to Caroline. "I'm not."

"Me neither," added Oliver. He was grinning from ear to ear.

RAE

I'm glad Caroline picked Treat. I'm going to put lots of whipped cream on my sundae. We're all kind of hoping Chef Gary falls down, but not to hurt himself, of course.

....

While the junior chefs waited at the ice cream table, Chef Gary was outfitted with safety gear—wrist guards, elbow pads, knee pads, and a helmet. When he was done, he raised his arms in a cheer, "I'M READY FOR ANYTHING!"

Chef Aimee smiled and looked at her watch. "Start your sundaes!" Two minutes later she gave Chef Gary a little push, "GO!"

Chef Gary inched forward, slowly at first, but then faster and faster. It was a straight shot to the ice cream station— no turns. Caroline saw Chef Gary approaching and quickly added her finishing touch—one maraschino cherry on top of a swirl of whipped cream. When she turned to look again, her eyes widened. Chef Gary was NOT slowing down.

He waved his arms. "Move! MOVE! Coming in HOT! HOT! HOT!" Caroline jumped to the side just in time. He body-slammed into the table. *CRASH!*

"OW!" He looked up. "Sorry!"

Rae stifled a giggle.

Chef Gary put the sundaes on a tray, took a deep breath, and pushed off toward the obstacle course. He weaved slowly in and out between the first few cones. Holding the tray while skating was not easy, but soon he was picking up speed. Fast was not better—it was hard to control the skates. He missed two of the turns and plowed right over one of the orange cones. His skates crossed the finish line a moment later.

Chef Aimee clapped and cheered, but Chef Gary didn't stop. He was speeding across the parking lot toward the other side. He hit the curb and was suddenly airborne. A second later, he belly-flopped onto the grass, arms out like a giant starfish. There was a horrified silence. Then slowly a hand rose up. "I'm okay!"

"YAY!" Everyone cheered.

Chef Gary sat up. He was covered in whipped cream, chocolate sauce, and sprinkles. He pulled off the skates and threw them into the bushes. "That's it for skating!"

They cheered again.

Chef Gary is amazing! He's not afraid of trying new things, even if it makes him look silly. He's an inspiration. I'm pretty sure everyone is glad I picked Treat!

CAROLINE

CHAPTER 8

liver was chatty at breakfast. Rae studied him. Considering he'd lost yesterday, this was a surprise. Where was his usual scowl of disappointment? Maybe he knew something about today's challenge. It wasn't fair to keep secrets. Not when they had the pact. She pushed the muffin basket across the table. "Why so happy? Do you know something we don't?" She raised her eyebrows.

Caroline leaned forward and said in a low voice, "STP! Stick-together pact! Remember? STP!"

Oliver dug out a blueberry muffin. "Okay, but it's not what you're thinking. It's personal . . ." He looked around the room. "And kind of weird."

The girls leaned in.

"My mom makes me do this thing called visualization. It's a brain exercise. You know, where you imagine a thing you want, like our food trucks."

Caroline shook her head.

"What? How?" Rae looked confused.

Oliver sighed. "Okay, so I imagine my food truck, walking up to it, what it looks like inside. That kind of thing. My mom says it's supposed to help me have a winning spirit or something. I told you, it's weird, but it kind of works. It makes me feel positive and focused."

Rae stared, not sure what to say. This was not what she was expecting.

"Huh!" Caroline nodded. "Maybe we'll try it too." She looked at Rae and exaggerated her nodding. "So we can all be even."

Rae took the hint. "Yes, thank you for sharing."

"Whatever." Oliver looked away and bit the muffin.

••••

After breakfast, it was time for some quick interviews. Today's theme was comfort food. How hard could that be? Caroline led the way to the filming studio, but instead of stopping at the orange door and waiting for the others, she knocked and went right in.

Oliver and Rae exchanged surprised glances.

"What's up with her?" asked Oliver.

Rae shrugged.

Oliver gestured impatiently. "Well, I wanted to go first! Something's going on—she's different. It's like she's suddenly better at stuff."

Rae shrugged again, but she'd noticed.

My favorite comfort food is lasagna, but only the way my mom makes it. First she makes a ratatouille, and then she uses that as one of the layers. And instead of mozzarella cheese, she uses goat cheese in a béchamel sauce. It's amazing!

The minute Caroline stepped out of the interview room, Oliver pushed in front to take her place. Rae sighed and let him pass. The stick-together pact didn't make Oliver any less annoying.

Caroline pointed to the door. "The producer is a lot nicer than he used to be."

"Really?"

Caroline nodded. "I don't think he's trying to trick us into saying nasty things about each other anymore. That was probably just a last-week thing."

"Maybe," said Rae. But she wasn't so sure.

My favorite comfort food is fried chicken and biscuits, but it takes a long time to make. My aunt Laura shared her family recipe with me. You have to brine the chicken in buttermilk and spices. And the biscuits have to be made with cold butter, not shortening. A real chef knows that good ingredients make a difference.

When Oliver was done, Rae took her place on the stool. "Ready?" asked Steve.

The cameraman turned on the camera.

RAE

My favorite comfort food is my grandma's chicken pie. Before we started cooking, she used to buy biscuits for the top. The kind that come in a tube, and you have to whack it on the counter to get it to open. I always liked doing that part, but now we make our own. It takes longer, but it tastes better. Just smelling it baking makes me feel warm and happy.

Caroline and Oliver chatted nonstop all the way back to the lodge. Rae was there, right next to them, but she didn't say much. She was too busy thinking. The competition felt different. Just yesterday, they'd all been on equal ground, but today something had shifted.

CHAPTER 9

After lunch, they marched to the school studio.

At first it was just a joke. "Time to march over to the studio," said Chef Nancy, but then Oliver started calling out the pace and they really were marching. *ONE, TWO! ONE, TWO!* Even Chef Nancy joined in.

By the time they walked through the door, Rae was feeling better. One, two, one, two—that's what she needed to do. Take the competition one step at a time.

Caroline looked around. "No cameras!"

"Well, not for now," said Chef Nancy. "But there'll be interviews after the lesson."

Caroline shrugged. "You know what? I don't even care about the cameras anymore."

Chef Nancy walked to the big table at the front of the room. "There are two parts to this lesson. First we'll go over the five basic sauces and then we'll have a mini-challenge. Who can name the five basic sauces?"

"Espagnole, veloute, béchamel, tomato, and hollandaise!" said Oliver.

Chef Nancy nodded. "And not including taste, what is the most important quality of a sauce?"

Rae and Oliver both raised their hands.

"A stable emulsion!" shouted Oliver. "When one liquid becomes evenly dispersed inside another liquid."

Rae scowled. Why did he even bother putting his hand up if he was just going to yell out the answer?

"Correct, Oliver." Chef Nancy held up four fingers. "Four of these sauces start the same way. What is that common element?"

"A roux!" answered Caroline.

Rae spun around, surprised. This was suddenly a competition, and she wasn't getting any of the answers.

"Very good, Caroline. A roux is a paste that is used as a thickener for sauces. There are only two ingredients: flour, and butter or an animal fat.

Chef Nancy pulled on an apron. "Sauces! I could talk about them all day, but there just isn't time. How do we fix a sauce that's too thin?"

"Cornstarch!" answered Rae. "Mix cornstarch and water together and add that to the sauce. Or you can add rice, and then once it's cooked, purée the whole sauce."

"Or puréed tomato," offered Oliver. "One tablespoon at a time."

"Huh." Caroline looked at Oliver. "I didn't know that."

Chef Nancy nodded. "How about a sauce that's too thick?"

That was an easy one. Oliver, Rae, and Caroline all answered together. "More stock!"

Chef Nancy crisscrossed the apron strings behind and her back and tied them in front. "How would you fix a dish that's too salty?"

"Add water . . . no." Rae shook her head. "That would take too long, and you'd have to wait for it to reduce."

"Add cream?" asked Caroline.

Oliver raised his hand. "You could try a little sugar, but I'd use lemon juice! Acid can help to mask salt."

Rae stared. How did he know all these tricks? Did he study textbooks?

Chef Nancy smiled. "Very good, Oliver, and don't forget vinegar—it does the same thing."

"Okay!" Chef Nancy clapped her hands. "She pulled three bowls out from under the table and handed one to each of them. "I've given you each a hollandaise sauce. As you can see it's lumpy and watery. What should we do? How should we fix it?"

Caroline started to answer. Chef Nancy raised her hand. "No! Don't tell me. Show me. This will be a fast mini-challenge. Your workstations have been stocked with eggs, flour, and milk. I want you to fix this sauce and turn it into a smooth, creamy hollandaise. First one to achieve this wins. Okay, back to your workstations."

Caroline smiled. She knew exactly what to do. And she didn't stop smiling, not even when the cameras arrived.

"Ready?" asked Chef Nancy, but she didn't wait for an answer. "Let's get cooking!"

Caroline strained out the lumps and put the remaining sauce into a saucepan on low heat. She warmed a bowl with hot water, cracked an egg, and dropped the egg yolk into the bowl. Now all she had to do was whisk the yolk and slowly add the heated sauce.

"FINISHED!" Oliver threw his hands up.

Caroline dropped her whisk. WHAT? How could he be done so fast?

Chef Nancy picked up Oliver's bowl and swirled a spoon through the thick smooth hollandaise. "Well done, Oliver. Anyone else?"

Caroline and Rae both shook their heads.

Chef Nancy handed the bowl back. "Oliver, can you explain your process?"

"Yes, ma'am. I heated the mixture very slowly and using a whisk, I mixed in two teaspoons of boiling water, one drop at a time."

Rae couldn't believe it. "What? That's it?"

"Were you using the egg yolk method?" asked Chef Nancy.

Rae nodded.

"That works too," said Chef Nancy.

"It just takes longer," added Oliver. He smirked. "It's good to know the fast tricks."

While Oliver was at the Gadget Wall picking out his prize, Chef Nancy pulled out the black board. Whoever earned the most stars would get an advantage in the elimination challenge. Rae turned away. No need to watch—she wasn't getting a star. The space under her name was staying one hundred percent blank.

The difference between winning and losing is huge. It's pretty simple: winning feels like being on top of the mountain. I always want the good feeling. Who wouldn't? So I do everything I can to be better—that's not a crime.

OLIVER

Oliver came back from the Gadget Wall with a handheld citrus juicer. He put it in his toolbox.

"Getting pretty full," he bragged.

Chef Nancy pointed to the door. "Okay! Back to the lodge!"

••••

Rae couldn't wait to get Caroline alone. Now that they were in their room for the night, there were things she needed to know. "How did you do it?"

"Do what?" asked Caroline.

"Change so you wouldn't be nervous or scared of the cameras."

Caroline leaned forward. "You can tell?"

Rae nodded.

Caroline shifted uneasily. "I don't know. It was kind of like a switch: one minute I was a nervous person and then I wasn't. And now that I'm not, everything is easier."

"Huh." Rae slouched back against her pillow. She'd been hoping for more of a recipe—something she could follow too.

Caroline waved her arm. "Wait—it could have been the eggplant!"

"Eggplant?" Rae sat up.

"Yeah, remember the eggplant napoleon I made in the elimination challenge last week? That's the first time it happened. Getting the idea to make it was like a ZAP! My brain was suddenly on fire. Maybe that's all it takes. One good thing, and then you feel better about everything else, too. There should be a word for that kind of thing."

Rae leaned back and put her head on the pillow. She knew the word, but she didn't say it.

Caroline watched her. "Are you going to sleep?"

"Uh-huh." Rae snuggled under the covers.

She closed her eyes and imagined the Crafty Café, her fantasy food truck. If visualizing worked for Oliver, maybe it would work for her, too. She opened the door and looked inside. There was only one thing she was hoping to find: confidence.

CHAPTER 10

hef Nancy did not rush them through breakfast. "Take your time, enjoy. We don't need to be in the filming studio until this afternoon." It felt strange to have a morning of free time. Rae made three new clay charms, Caroline read magazines, and Oliver went to the library to look at recipe books. By lunchtime they were all restless.

They finished lunch in record time and were ready and waiting when Chef Nancy reappeared to take them to the filming studio.

Caroline moved up next to Chef Nancy. "You know how I won the Diner Challenge? When do they take my picture for the magazine?"

"Not sure," answered Chef Nancy, "but sometime before Thursday."

She whispered her next question. It was the one she really wanted to know. "Are Chef Gary and Chef Aimee going to name their puppy Freckles?"

Chef Nancy shrugged. "I don't know. We'll have to ask about that."

Oliver nudged Rae. "Remember the interview question about comfort food? I bet that's the next challenge."

Rae nodded. Of course it was. Why hadn't she thought of that?

Steve was waiting outside the studio door. He looked at Chef Nancy and tapped his watch.

"I know! I know! I'm sorry!" She held the door and waved everyone in. "Hurry! Line up behind the table. Chef Gary and Chef Porter are waiting."

As soon as everyone was in position, Steve gave the signal. "ROLLING!"

"Good afternoon and welcome back!" Chef Gary studied the junior chefs. "Are you rested and eager for a new challenge?"

"YES, CHEF!"

He smiled. "I'm ready too! And I really like this one."

Rae shot Caroline a nervous glance, but Caroline didn't notice.

Chef Porter moved toward the table. "Comfort food. What does that mean?" Oliver's hand shot up, but she ignored him. "It's food that makes us feel loved. It's food we share with our families. It's food that feels special and meaningful." Chef Porter clasped her hands together. "I want to thank you for sharing your family recipes with us. This is a privilege." She stepped back and Chef Gary took over.

"Thank you, Chef Porter. I feel the same." He turned toward the junior chefs. "I want to hear more about your comfort meals." He pointed to Rae. "Can you tell us about the chicken pot pie you and your grandmother make?"

"There are four parts to this recipe." She held up four fingers. "Part one is you have to cook your chicken. We usually roast it in the morning. Part two is you have to make the filling: we use onions, carrots, celery, potatoes, mushrooms, frozen peas, and spices and create a sauce using a white roux. Part three is the biscuits. Cheddar cheese and lots of pepper make them extra tasty."

Chef Gary nodded. "Sounds tasty and—"

"Delicious!" added Rae.

Chef Gary wiggled his fingers. "Part four?"

"Oops!" Rae blushed. "Baking. Part four is you have to put it all together—the chicken, the filling, and the biscuits on top—and then bake it."

"Thank you, Rae. That sounds like a very comforting dish."

Chef Porter turned to Oliver.

Of course, Oliver was ready with his answer. He wouldn't make a mistake like she'd done. Rae didn't pay attention. She heard random words: "buttermilk," "brine," "eight hours," "extra buttermilk," but her mind was too busy to listen. Seven words were on a continuous loop in her brain. *If you want it, make it happen. If you want it, make it happen.* It was her grandmother's saying, and hearing it was like pot pie—comforting.

She half listened to Caroline's description of her lasagna, but then . . . Wait! What did Chef Gary just say? She looked up. Everyone was staring at her.

"So," asked Chef Gary. "What do you think? Our little Uma is a real diva, and the name suites her perfectly!"

Rae eyes widened. "You named the puppy Uma?"

Chef Gary nodded. "Of course—that's what I just said."

Rae hugged her arms together and grinned. If the table hadn't been in the way, she might have hugged Chef Gary, too.

Caroline and Oliver looked disappointed.

Chef Porter tapped her wrist. There wasn't a watch, but Chef Gary got the hint.

"Okay, time to move on. As you may have guessed, today's challenge is comfort food. We're going to give you five minutes in the pantry to gather your ingredients, and then you'll have ninety minutes. Are you ready?"

"YES, CHEF!"

Rae smiled. Her favorite meal and the puppy surprise—her luck was definitely changing!

"CUT!" yelled Steve.

"Workstations!" shouted Chef Nancy.

OLIVER

There are two things you absolutely *have* to do to make good fried chicken. Brine and bake! The baking part is kind of a secret. After frying the chicken you put it in the oven for ten minutes. But how can I brine if I only have ninety minutes? I'm going to have to improvise, and it's not going to be easy.

"Five minutes to make a list!" announced Chef Nancy. "And then we'll be back on camera for the pantry run."

Caroline quickly scribbled out a list of ingredients: eggplants, zucchini, tomatoes, onions, peppers, and thyme for the ratatouille, and flour and eggs for the lasagna noodles. Homemade noodles were a must, but that wasn't going to be hard. She'd made them before.

There isn't a trick to making this lasagna. You just have to be patient—the ratatouille has to cook down so that all the flavors meld together. It's the difference between tasting good and tasting great. I'm glad we have ninety minutes. I can work with that.

CAROLINE

Chef Nancy made a tour of the workstations. "Remember your lists. There's no going back. You don't want to forget anything."

Rae carefully taped the list to the inside of her basket. On TV it would look like she'd memorized all her ingredients, but that wasn't true. The list was handy, if she needed it.

RAE

Chicken pot pie isn't that hard to make if you have a lot of time, but we only have ninety minutes, so I'll have to rush. The first thing I'll do is poach the chicken breasts. Poaching is not the same as boiling—it's more delicate. If you simmer the breasts in a broth of herbs and spices, they'll be moist and flavorful. Boiling would make them rubbery.

Chef Nancy ran to the front of the room and clapped her hands. "Places, everyone!"

"ROLLING!" shouted Steve.

Chef Gary's hand sliced the air. "GO!"

It was a race to the pantry. Mark and Janet moved in for camera close-ups, but everyone was too busy to notice.

Five minutes passed quickly.

"TIME!" called Chef Gary.

Rae ran to her workstation. Something was wrong. Where was Steve? He always called *CUT* right after the pantry run, but today he just stood off to the side, smiling.

Chef Gary stepped forward. "We can't wait to try these delicious recipes, but I hope you've been listening to each other, because we have a twist. You are NOT going to make your own comfort food dish. You're going to switch baskets!"

Caroline looked at Rae, Oliver looked at Caroline, and a shiver swept down Rae's spine.

Chef Porter held up the green bag. "Oliver, since you were the winner of the last challenge, you may pick a name from the bag."

Oliver walked to the front of the room, picked out an envelope, and handed it to Chef Porter.

Rae held her breath. She was in trouble. BIG TROUBLE! She hadn't listened to Caroline and Oliver explain their meals. She had no idea how to make ratatouille—in fact, she'd never even heard of it before. She crossed her fingers. If she got Oliver's basket, maybe at least she'd have a chance.

Chef Porter opened the envelope. "Congratulations, Oliver. You will be making Caroline's ratatouille and Caroline will make Rae's chicken pot pie, and Rae will make Oliver's fried chicken."

Rae breathed a fast sigh of relief, but it didn't last—she was nervous again.

Chef Gary picked up Oliver's basket and placed it in front of Rae. "This is exciting. We can't wait to try your hearty home-cooked meals."

"CUT!" shouted Steve.

No one moved. Oliver, Caroline, and Rae stood motionless in stunned silence.

CHAPTER 11

Before the cameras started up again, Chef Nancy visited each contestant to give them tips and discuss cooking strategies. Oliver had an eggplant question, Caroline had a biscuit question, and Rae wanted to know which was better for frying—peanut oil or canola oil? Chef Nancy couldn't tell the junior chefs what to do, but she could share information so they could decide for themselves. "Peanut oil has a mild flavor and a smoking point of 450 degrees. Canola oil has a smoking point of 400 degrees."

Rae nodded. If the oil burnt, the fried chicken would be ruined. A higher smoking point would be better. Peanut oil was the winner.

"One minute!" Steve pointed to the cameras.

Chef Nancy stepped off to the side.

"ROLLING!" shouted Steve.

Chef Porter took center stage. She didn't raise her voice or her hand. "You have ninety minutes. Let's get cooking!"

Oliver grabbed the eggplants and began slicing. He had a plan, and he'd worked backwards to figure out the timing. The lasagna would take forty minutes to cook, the ratatouille would take twenty minutes to cook, plus there was the *mise en place,* but before he could even start on that, he had to salt and drain the eggplants. It was going to be a rush. He only had fifty minutes to get everything made and assembled.

My biggest challenge is the brining. I'm not an expert at it, but I do know that brining takes hours, not minutes. The meat needs time to absorb the buttermilk. If I don't brine, the chicken could be tough and dry. It'll take me twenty-five minutes to batter and fry the chicken, so that only leaves forty-five minutes for brining. I just hope that's enough.

RAE

Rae prepared her brine, mixing buttermilk, paprika, salt, hot sauce, garlic, rosemary, thyme, pepper, and a little lemon juice. She added the chicken, covered the bowl, and put it the refrigerator. Chef Porter arrived just as she was mixing up flour, baking soda, baking powder, and salt.

"Where are you in your process?"

Rae kept mixing. "I'm making biscuits and my chicken is brining in the refrigerator."

Chef Porter glanced around the room. "You seem calm. Are you comfortable with your assignment?"

Rae nodded. "Mostly. I've made biscuits before, but the fried chicken is new. I'll be super busy later. Once I start frying."

"Yes, you will!" Chef Porter lingered a minute to watch and then turned and headed toward Caroline.

"Hello, Caroline. What are you working on?"

Caroline pointed to the stove. "I'm poaching the chicken with thyme, rosemary, salt, pepper, and lemon slices. It'll be done in fifteen minutes."

"And what's this?" Chef Porter tapped the cutting board.

"Oh." Caroline picked up a knife. "It's for the chicken pie. I'm dicing parsnips, mushrooms, carrots, celery, and onions."

Chef Porter examined a small white cube. "Parsnips instead of potatoes—that's interesting."

Caroline felt a slight wave of panic. Was that good or bad? "It wasn't my idea. They were in Rae's basket."

"Of course," said Chef Porter. "Carry on." And then she was gone.

CAROLINE

My biggest challenge is getting everything ready fast enough so I can get it all put together and into the oven to bake. The pie needs to bake for twenty-five minutes, so that gives me an hour of prep time. I can do it. It's a lot less complicated than my lasagna recipe. Oliver has way more to do.

Chef Gary approached Oliver just as he was adding crushed tomatoes to a pan.

"What's cooking?"

"Tomatoes, peppers, and onions," answered Oliver. He stirred the mixture together. "And when this is cooked, I'll add back the cooked eggplant and zucchini."

Chef Gary nodded. "Patience is hard in a time crunch, but a good ratatouille takes time."

"That's okay." Oliver grabbed a ball of dough and started to knead. "It gives me time to make the noodles."

"Nice job, Oliver. It looks like you've got everything under control."

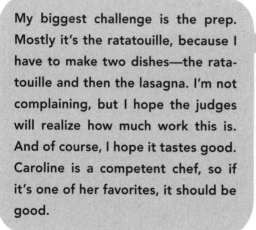

My biggest challenge is the prep. Mostly it's the ratatouille, because I have to make two dishes—the ratatouille and then the lasagna. I'm not complaining, but I hope the judges will realize how much work this is. And of course, I hope it tastes good. Caroline is a competent chef, so if it's one of her favorites, it should be good.

OLIVER

"FORTY-FIVE MINUTES!" called Chef Gary.

CLANK! A pot crashed onto the floor.

Chef Gary rushed over to Oliver's workstation. "Is everything okay?"

Oliver answered without looking up. "I'm sorry, sir. Accident. Empty pot. I have to assemble this lasagna and get it into the oven NOW!" He covered the bottom of a mini loaf pan with noodles and then spooned on a layer of the ratatouille.

Chef Gary picked up the pot, put it on the table, and quietly moved away. Oliver didn't need help—he needed time.

"Thirty minutes!" announced Chef Porter.

Caroline opened the oven door, placed her pot pie on the middle rack, closed the door, and stepped back, breathing a sigh of relief. Now she could relax—all she had to do was wait. She looked around the room. Oliver caught her eye and nodded. He was waiting too.

They both watched Rae. Her biscuits were in the oven, but she wasn't waiting. The next thirty minutes would be a race against time. Rae pulled the chicken pieces out of the brine and set them on wire racks to drain, then poured peanut oil into a deep skillet and turned it on.

"While that gets hot, I'll make the breading." The room was quiet. Rae was the only one talking, but she didn't seem to notice. She added flour, salt, pepper, thyme, paprika, and cayenne pepper to a large bowl and mixed.

Chef Gary came over to watch. "How's it going?"

Rae added a small amount of buttermilk to her flour mixture. "I want the crust to stick and be crunchy so I'm making this coating a little lumpy on purpose. It's an experiment. I hope it works." She coated two pieces of chicken in the batter and carefully placed them in the hot oil using tongs.

Chef Gary nodded approvingly. "Nice work, Rae."

····

Everyone was busy at the end. Plating was important. The food had to look as good as it tasted.

Oliver nudged the lasagna out of the pan and onto the center of a large plate. It held together in a perfect mini rectangle. He arranged a display of thinly sliced fried eggplants and tomatoes in an artistic swirl around the edge.

Caroline scooped out a piece of the pie, careful to keep the biscuit intact. She placed it in the middle of a plate and decorated one edge with cooked carrots and parsnips cut to look like leaves.

Rae balanced her chicken on end, resting up against her golden brown biscuit. She added a tiny ramekin of spicy butter garnished with a nasturtium leaf.

"TIME!" called Chef Gary.

The hands went up.

"CUT!" yelled Steve.

"Five-minute break!" shouted Chef Nancy.

Rae, Oliver, and Caroline stood to the side while the camerapeople took close-ups of the food.

Caroline moved next to Rae. "I wonder if I made it the way you make it? If it tastes the same?"

Rae leaned over to look. "It looks good . . . but I won't get to taste it." She shrugged. "We'll never know."

CHAPTER 12

ow for my favorite part," said Chef Gary. "The tasting! We're proud of you. This wasn't easy, but you adapted well. Chef Porter and I can't wait to try the comfort dishes you've prepared. Caroline, will you please bring your plate to the table?"

Caroline walked to the front and set her plate down.

"Perfect golden brown crust on the biscuit," said Chef Porter.

"Nice presentation," said Chef Gary.

Chef Porter pointed to the leaves on the side of the plate. "Are these cooked?"

"Yes," answered Caroline, "you can eat them." She waited for Chef Porter to pick up one of the three forks, but she didn't. Caroline stared at the table. Three forks! Why were there three forks? Was Chef Aimee coming?

Chef Gary looked out into the room. "Rae, can you please join us?"

Caroline froze. Rae was the other fork!

Chef Gary handed out the forks. "We'll all take a bite at the same time. On three. One, two, three." Three forks attacked the pot pie.

"Flakey!" said Chef Porter. "I was right about the crust— it's just the right amount of crispy."

"And the chicken is tender," added Chef Gary.

Chef Porter licked her spoon. "The sauce is sophisticated. I like the bitterness. Nicely done."

Chef Gary looked at Rae. "So, what do you think? Does it taste like home? Be honest."

Rae shot an apologetic look at Caroline, then mumbled something under her breath.

"What was that?" asked Chef Gary. "Can you repeat it?"

"No, Chef, it doesn't taste like home."

"What's different?" asked Chef Porter.

"Parsnips," said Rae. "I don't like them. I usually only put in a tiny piece, because my grandma makes me. But this has a lot and no potatoes."

Caroline leaned forward. "Well, I didn't know that! There wasn't a recipe, plus there weren't any potatoes listed!"

Rae gasped and covered her mouth. "Oh no! I forgot the potatoes!"

"Well," said Chef Gary. "That's good to know and . . ."

"Well, I enjoyed the parsnips!" interrupted Chef Porter. She smiled at Caroline. "In fact I'm sure I preferred them over potatoes. It was very good."

"Thank you, Chef." Having Chef Porter on your side was like winning a special award. Caroline smiled, but not at Rae. It was hard to be judged by a good friend.

"Caroline, please stay here. Rae, you may go back to your workstation. Oliver, can you bring your plate to the table?"

Oliver carried up the lasagna and set it carefully on the table.

"How did you get that perfect rectangle?" asked Chef Gary.

Oliver sighed. "I was running out of time, and I knew the lasagna would cook faster in a smaller dish, so I used a mini loaf pan."

"Clever and attractive," said Chef Gary. "Good problem solving."

Chef Porter leaned in closer. "I like how it looks too. A comfort meal for one. I can't wait to try it. Ratatouille has always been one of my favorites, though this will be the first time . . . lasagna style."

Chef Gary handed Caroline a fork. "Are you ready?"

She nodded nervously. Being a judge was harder than being judged.

"Okay, forks in on three. One, two, three!" Everyone took a taste.

"*Oh!* Rich and savory!" said Chef Gary.

Chef Porter held up her fork. "And the texture of the noodles is al dente—not too soft, not too hard—perfect! Perhaps a little more goat cheese?"

Caroline nodded in agreement.

Chef Gary noticed. "So, Caroline, how does it compare?"

"It's almost the same, just more goat cheese and I like it better in a bigger pan, because I don't like crunchy noodles. I always ask for a middle piece."

Chef Porter shook her head. "Not me—I like how the noodles get crunchy on the edge, but everyone has their preference. Well done, Oliver!"

Oliver bowed his head. "Thank you, ma'am."

Chef Gary sent Caroline back to her workstation and called Rae to the front.

Rae stared at her plate. Oliver was going to rip her to shreds. Her biscuit was perfect, she knew that, but the fried chicken? She crossed her fingers. There was a lot that could be

wrong. It could be too dry, too crunchy, not crunchy enough, or even raw—raw would be the worst!

Chef Gary liked the presentation, and Chef Porter was excited to try the spicy butter, but their enthusiasm didn't help her feel any less anxious.

Instead of handing out forks, Chef Gary cut the biscuit and chicken into three pieces. Chef Gary counted to three and everyone took a bite.

"Spicy!"

"Flakey!"

Oliver didn't say a word.

Chef Gary took a bite of chicken. "Nice crust, but not very juicy."

Oliver smirked.

"That spicy butter is delicious," gushed Chef Porter. "But I have to agree with Chef Gary about the chicken—it's a little dry."

Oliver smiled.

Chef Gary turned to Oliver. "What do you think? Does it feel like home cooking?"

Oliver shook his head. "No, sir. But it's not Rae's fault. It's impossible to make my fried chicken in only ninety minutes. Not even I could do it, because the chicken needs to marinate in the brine for at least six hours."

Oliver popped a piece of biscuit into his mouth. "This biscuit, though—it's perfect!"

Chef Porter looked at Rae. "Well, what do you say to that?"

Rae forced an awkward grin. "Thank you?" Oliver had just saved her *and* given her a compliment. Why? Was it the stick-together pact?

How do I feel about the other competitors? I like them and trust them. This is a food competition only. What happens in the kitchen stays in the kitchen. Outside the kitchen we're friends. We watch out for each other. What Oliver said proves that.

RAE

Chef Gary and Chef Porter moved off to the side to discuss the competition.

When they came back, Chef Gary was holding a cookbook. "Many chefs do not use these, but as you have seen, a recipe can be of the upmost importance. Especially if you want to replicate a dish. This was not an easy challenge, but you impressed us with your determination and enthusiasm. Rae, your biscuits were standout delicious. Caroline, your pot pie was both homey and sophisticated. Oliver, your lasagna was a savory treat, and we were especially impressed by the creative way you solved the time issue for baking. The winner of this challenge is . . . Oliver!"

Rae was disappointed, but not surprised. She'd win next time—she just had to—she was in last place.

Oliver smiled and walked to the front. Everyone clapped. Even Rae.

CHAPTER 14

C hef Nancy stood at the head of the breakfast table. "It's a full day today. Lots to do. Breakfast, interviews, and then we'll head on our field trip to the Sunnyside Food Pantry. We'll be volunteering, and then there's a tour with the onsite manager. The cameras will be with us, so everyone needs to be on their best behavior. We'll come back for lunch, and then continue with the activities marked on the schedule: a challenge and a lesson."

Rae sat up, attentive. "That *is* a lot."

"Absolutely," agreed Chef Nancy. "So eat a good breakfast—you'll need the energy. Interviews start in fifteen minutes."

I've never been to a food pantry before, so I'm looking forward to seeing how it works, and helping out, of course.

OLIVER

I've donated food to the food pantry, but I haven't visited the actual place where people go to get the food. It's sad that people don't have enough to eat, so I feel really good that we are going to help and be part of it.

CAROLINE

RAE

I've been to the food pantry before. I went with my dad a few times to get a box of food. The people there were really nice. It was kind of like shopping in a super-small grocery store, only there weren't as many choices. I'm glad that I get to help out.

They piled into a van and twenty minutes later pulled into the parking lot.

Caroline looked around, confused. "I thought we were going to a store. Where is it?"

Chef Nancy pointed to a big square industrial warehouse. "It's inside there. They need a big space so they can organize and store all the food donations."

Sophia the onsite manager met them at the big open garage door. "Thank you for coming! We're so excited to have you."

Sophia led them into the warehouse, where boxes and

cans were organized on shelves. "We get these donations from stores, individuals, and corporations." She pointed to a large group of boxes in the middle of the room. "And these are the boxes you'll be sorting. We sort them out so it's faster to stock the store. Let me show you the sorting bins." She led them on a tour of the room, pointing out the various bins. "Dry soup bin, canned soup bin, bean bin, snack bin, candy bin, vegetable bin, fruit bin, chili bin, and juice bin. It's pretty simple: you open the box, sort the contents into the various bins, flatten the box, and then put it in the recycling area. It's usually faster to work as a team, but I'll let you decide how to split things up." Sophia pointed to a long, narrow hallway. "Chef Nancy and I will be in the store area at the other end. If you need anything, just come and find us. We'll check back in an hour."

Chef Nancy followed Sophia down the hall, then turned for one last wave to the contestants.

"What now?" asked Caroline. "There's probably a hundred boxes."

Mark and Janet stood off to the side, filming.

Oliver opened a box and pulled out two cans. "We get started." He walked toward the soup bin.

"Wait!" Rae waved her hands. "If we work together, it might go faster. We could each do a different job—like an assembly line."

It was a good plan and soon they had efficient rhythm of unpacking and sorting.

Caroline dropped five boxes into the snack bin. "It's kind of fun. How many boxes left?"

Oliver stopped to count. "Twenty-three."

Rae looked at the clock. "If we speed it up, we might be able to finish before Chef Nancy gets back."

"Let's do it!" shouted Caroline.

It was close, they almost didn't make it. Oliver was just flattening the last box when Chef Nancy and Sophia walked up.

"WOW!" Sophia stared at the empty space in the middle of the room. "I can't believe you finished!"

"Teamwork!" said Oliver.

Caroline and Rae moved next to him and smiled. Janet moved in for a close-up.

Chef Nancy motioned for them to follow her. "Let's visit the store."

••••

When they got to the store, only Rae stepped inside. Oliver and Caroline watched from the entrance.

Rae walked down the aisle. "This is pretty nice."

"Thank you," said Sophia. "We like to think so."

Caroline pushed past Oliver to follow Rae. "I thought it would look like a real store, but it doesn't. It looks home-made."

Rae nodded. "Yeah, but look! They have fresh fruit and vegetables. That's pretty unusual. Plus, there's a dairy section and a baking section! This is a good pantry."

"How do you know so much about food pantries?" asked Caroline.

Rae wasn't sure how to answer, but Chef Nancy saved her. She stepped to the center of the room and waved a can of green beans in the air.

"How can we make these delicious?"

Everyone had a different answer.

"Add butter and sprinkle with Parmesan."

"Stir fry with sesame oil and garlic."

"Purée with butter, cream, cheese, salt, and pepper."

"Wonderful! Wonderful!" Sophia clapped her hands. "I'm going to write those down for our customers, and I might try them too!" She followed the group outside to the van. "Thank you for all your help today!"

"We enjoyed it," said Chef Nancy. She opened the door. Everyone got in except Rae. She ran back to Sophia for a hug. "Thank you!"

And then it was back to Porter Farms!

CHAPTER 15

Caroline, Oliver, and Rae sat at the big table in lodge, eating lunch. Soon they'd be heading to the filming studio for a challenge.

Caroline nibbled her sandwich. "I never really knew what a food pantry was. I'm sort of feeling guilty about eating this sandwich."

Rae shook her head. "That's silly! No one at a food pantry would be jealous of a sandwich! Now, if it was your fancy lasagna—that's different."

Caroline smiled and took a bite. "I guess so, but it makes me feel lucky."

Rae nodded. "We are lucky, and that's good not to forget."

····

Fifteen minutes later they were in the filming studio.

"We'll start at the front table," said Chef Nancy. "Chef Gary and Chef Aimee want to talk with you."

"ROLLING!" shouted Steve.

Chef Gary put a paper bag on the table. "Did you enjoy helping at the food pantry?"

"Yes, Chef!"

Chef Aimee opened the bag, pulled out three cans of soup and read the titles as she lined them up on the table. "Tomato soup, cream of mushroom soup, and cream of chicken soup."

"Look familiar?" asked Chef Gary.

The young chefs all nodded.

Chef Gary rubbed his hands. "You worked well together at the pantry, so we thought we'd give you another assignment as a group."

Rae shot a worried look at Oliver. Sorting boxes together was not the same as cooking together.

"We want you to create a comfort meal that can replicated by someone who shops at the pantry. This meal will include a main dish, a side dish, and a dessert. Each dish must include a can of soup. What you make will be up to you, and which soup you use will also be your choice."

Chef Aimee pointed to the pantry. "Our pantry has been limited to include only those items that you might find at a food pantry. You will have ten minutes to explore the pantry, decide on your soup, and discuss your meal plan. When you return, you'll have sixty minutes to make your dish. Your time starts NOW!"

Nobody moved.

"NOW!" shouted Chef Gary.

Rae grabbed Caroline's hand and took off for the pantry. Oliver followed close behind.

Caroline stood in the center of the small room and spun in a slow circle. "There's nothing here! Everything's gone! What are we supposed to cook with?"

Rae nodded. Caroline wasn't exaggerating. Most of the shelves looked empty.

Oliver pulled out a pen and a small notebook. "We need to make a list of what's here! Then we can decide what to make." He walked to one of the shelves and got started.

Cake mix, corn muffin mix, spices, salt, pepper, corn flaked cereal, canned corn, chili, canned green beans, peanut butter, sugar, canned pinto beans, tortilla chips, canned tomato sauce, ketchup, jam.

Caroline ran to the fridge and listed off what she saw, "Chicken breasts, cheddar cheese, Parmesan cheese, milk, butter, eggs, cottage cheese, and cream cheese."

Rae covered the fresh produce: "Onions and potatoes."

"Really? That's all?" Caroline came to look for herself. "Not even fresh garlic?"

"Nope."

"What about the dessert?" complained Rae. "Dessert from soup—that's impossible."

Oliver pointed his pen. "Don't worry, I got that covered. My grandma makes a tomato soup cake—I'll just have to improvise a bit."

"That leaves chicken soup and mushroom soup," said Caroline.

A minute later, everything was decided. They ran back to the big table smiling.

"Welcome back," said Chef Aimee. "Are you ready?"

"YES, CHEF!"

"Wow, so excited. That makes me happy. You may choose your can of soup and proceed to your workstations."

Steve watched until all the contestants were in place and then, "CUT!"

"Interview time!" announced Chef Nancy. "And then we'll get started."

OLIVER

I chose the tomato soup. The tomato is actually a fruit, so it's not that much of a stretch to make a dessert with it. I'm going to make tomato soup spice cake. The tomato soup keeps the cake moist. Normally I'd use home-made ingredients, but we just don't have those kind of supplies today.

I chose the cream of chicken soup for my side dish. I'm making a baked cheesy corn casserole. I've never used canned soup in a recipe before. This will be a first. I hope it works out.

CAROLINE

RAE

I chose the cream of mushroom soup for my entrée. I'm going to make a mushroom, potato, and chicken casserole. Fresh mushrooms would have been a big help, but the pantry didn't have any. That's what people who shop at the pantry feel like—happy to have the food, but wishing there were more choices.

Chef Nancy stepped to the center of the room. "I will not be coming around to visit you today—you're on your own."

There wasn't time to think about this new twist, because the minute Chef Nancy was gone, Chef Gary gave the signal to start. "Let's get cooking!"

Oliver mixed milk and eggs and the can of soup in a bowl. In another bowl he added cinnamon to the cake mix, then added this to his egg mixture. He buttered and floured a cake pan and spooned in the batter.

Chef Aimee arrived just as he was popping the pan into the oven. "Done already?"

Oliver nodded. "It's fast when you use premade items, but I still have to make icing."

Chef Aimee looked at the clock. "More than enough time—forty minutes left." She moved over to see Rae.

Rae was using a mandolin to slice her potatoes.

"How is it going?"

"Crazy!" answered Rae. "There's so much to do and not much cooking time. I pounded the chicken breasts to make them thinner so they'd cook faster, and now I'm sautéing the onions and slicing potatoes both at the same time."

"How are you putting it together?" ask Chef Aimee.

Rae pulled out a baking dish. "I'll layer the potatoes, put the chicken on top, and then cover them both with the mushroom soup and the onions."

"Sounds tasty," said Chef Aimee. "Are you confident?"

"Confident!" Rae held up her potato.

Caroline was Chef Aimee's last stop. She looked around at the empty pots and pans. "Oh no, did I miss everything?"

Caroline pointed to the oven. "The cheesy corn casserole is baking. I just have to make the topping."

Chef Aimee looked through the oven window. "Looks good."

"TEN MINUTES LEFT!"

Oliver pulled his cake out of the oven and placed it on a rack. There was no way it would cool in time for frosting, so instead he improvised a glaze in a double boiler, quickly heating sugar, cream cheese, and milk.

Caroline and Rae and Oliver worked together to plate their meal. They placed their dishes on a long wooden cutting board. Three small single-serving plates—one for each menu item. Oliver sliced three thin pieces of cake and stacked them together. Rae gathered the mushrooms from the sauce and arranged them in a line next to the chicken breast. She added a saucy swirl to the edge of the plate. Caroline sprinkled crushed cornflakes on top and down one side of her ramekin.

"TIME!" Six hands flew into the air.

"CUT!"

The hands came down.

Steve motioned for Janet and Mark to follow him. "Let's get those close-ups."

CHAPTER 16

Chef Gary called everyone to the front.

Oliver set the board on the table. Rae and Caroline stood at his side.

Chef Gary looked at the table, then the group. "Look at this. You work well together." He pointed to Rae. "Tell us, about your dish."

"It's a chicken potato bake with a mushroom onion gravy."

Chef Gary nodded. "That sounds like comfort food to me." He handed forks and knives to Chef Aimee and Chef Nancy. "Let's dig in."

"Mmm, this is really good," said Chef Nancy. "I have a sweet spot for mushrooms."

Chef Aimee nodded. "Me too. And the chicken is moist and tender."

Chef Gary speared a potato and popped it into his mouth. "Nice sauce, and the potato is firm but cooked. Well done, Rae. How did you find this challenge?"

Rae shook her head. "Challenging! It's not easy to cook when you don't have many supplies and hardly any fresh food."

"So true," said Chef Gary. "And yet for many people this is a reality."

Chef Aimee pulled Caroline's dish to the center of the table. "Caroline, tell us about your dish."

"It's a cheesy baked corn casserole."

Chef Gary tried a bite. "It's like cornbread, but moist and cheesy. And I love the crunchy bits on top. What are they?"

Caroline smiled nervously. "It's kind of an invention— they're crispy fried onions and smashed cornflakes mixed together."

"Really?" Chef Aimee took another bite. "Wow, I'd never have guessed. That is an invention."

Oliver was the last to present. "I made a tomato soup spiced cake."

Chef Aimee picked up a clean fork. "How did you come up with that?"

Oliver shook his head. "It wasn't really my idea. My grandma makes something kind of similar."

Chef Aimee took a bite. "Nice, but not very spicy. I only taste cinnamon."

Oliver nodded. "I wanted to add cloves, but there weren't any in the pantry."

"Unfortunate," said Chef Gary. "But sometimes you just have to make do."

"I still like it," said Chef Nancy. "It's not overly sweet, even with the glaze."

"And it's very moist," added Chef Aimee. "Nice job, Oliver."

....

Oliver, Rae, and Caroline waited while the judges stepped off to the side to discuss the competition. Two minutes later they were back at the table.

Chef Gary waved a stack of papers. "We are proud of all of you. Even with restrictions, you were able to create interesting, delicious, and creative dishes. We'd like you to share your recipes with the food pantry, so when we're done here, please write them down." He dropped the papers onto the table. "The winner of today's challenge really did some out-of-the-box thinking, and that was impressive. Caroline, please step forward—you are the winner. Your corn casserole was delicious, but it was the unconventional topping that really impressed us. Congratulations!"

"Thank you, Chef!"

Chef Aimee pointed to the Gadget Wall. "Caroline, you may pick out your prize."

Chef Nancy added another star to the black board. Caroline and Oliver had two stars each. They were tied in the race for the Golden Envelope advantage.

Caroline bounced all the way to the Gadget Wall and came back holding a hand mixer. "Look!"

"I'm happy for you," said Rae, and she meant it.

CHAPTER 17

It was lesson time in the filming studio.

Chef Nancy clasped her hands in front of her heart. "We are now going to make the most delicious thing ever invented . . . dulce de leche!" She paused for a moment. "It's a sweet sauce with origins in Argentina, but many Latin American countries are famous for having their own variations. You can put it in ice cream, cakes, cookies, bars, and my personal favorite—you can eat it with a spoon."

"It's caramel," said Caroline.

Chef Nancy shook her head. "No, that's a common misconception. Dulce de leche is *not* caramel. Caramel is a mixture of water and sugar, while dulce de leche is whole milk, sugar, vanilla, and a tiny bit of baking soda. The only thing needed to change these four ingredients into pure deliciousness is time, and we're going to need a lot of that. Dulce de leche takes three hours to make."

"What?" Rae couldn't believe it.

Chef Nancy smiled. "Don't worry, it'll be worth it." Chef Nancy handed out the recipes and sent everyone back to their workstations. "Mix the ingredients together in a saucepan and set it on low heat. Then you're going to stir until the sugar's dissolved. For the first ninety minutes, you'll want to stir it regularly. The last hour will be the most critical. As your sauce thickens and changes to a dark golden brown, there's more chance of it burning. There's only one rule in this process: STIR!"

Caroline raised her hand. "Is this a mini-challenge?"

Chef Nancy paused for a minute. "No one will be taste testing your dulce de leche today."

Once the dulce de leches were mixed and cooking, Chef Nancy started a lesson on baking.

She pointed at Oliver. "What's the number one rule for dulce de leche?"

"STIR!"

Chef Nancy nodded. "Very good, Oliver. We're doing two things at once here, baking lesson and dulce de leche, so please feel free to check your pots and . . ."

". . . STIR!" They all said it together.

••••

Chef Nancy handed out the ingredients for a pie crust: flour, sugar, salt, butter, apple cider vinegar, ice water, and a pie plate.

Caroline wiggled her fingers. "Everything's so cold, even the flour."

"That's on purpose!" said Chef Nancy. "Because the colder your ingredients, the better chance for a successful pie crust. Let's do this together. Step one: stir your flour, sugar, and salt together in your bowl." She waited until they were done, then continued. "Step two: cut your butter into small pieces and mix it into your flour with a pastry cutter." She glanced around the room. "Is it crumbly like tiny pebbles?"

"Yes, Chef!"

"Step three: using one tablespoon at time, mix in the vinegar and just enough cold water so that your mixture forms into a ball. Be careful not to overwork the dough. Overmixing will make your crust tough." Chef Nancy stopped and surveyed everyone's progress. "Normally I'd suggest you let the dough sit for at least forty minutes in the refrigerator, but we don't have time to sit around and wait."

Caroline snuck a little piece of dough off the side of her ball and popped it into her mouth.

Rae's eyes widened, but she didn't say anything.

Chef Nancy surveyed the room. "Do you like surprises? How about a mini-challenge?" There was only one answer.

"Yes, Chef!"

Chef Nancy handed out apple pie filling and pie plates. "We have pre-chilled some dough for you to use, so let's swap out the dough you just made. Don't worry, this challenge is about design, not taste."

"ROLLING!" shouted Steve.

Chef Nancy continued: "Family is a recurring theme this

week, so we're asking you to create an original design that is reflective of your family. You will have twenty minutes for this challenge." Chef Nancy raised her hand. "And your time starts now!"

"Aaaah!" Rae didn't usually complain out loud, but surprise challenges were hard. Your brain had to switch gears super fast.

Oliver separated his dough into two balls and floured the surface of his table. The top crust would be the important one, so while he was thinking of an idea, he'd make the bottom crust and fill the pie. Oliver rolled out the ball, working from the center, then lifted the edge to be sure it wasn't sticking. He wasn't a pie expert, but he knew that the less you handled the dough, the better.

> Every challenge is important, so you really have to be smart about the decisions you make. Family means togetherness, comfort, and support. I'm going to use that as a starting point for my design. There won't be any hearts—my pie will be sophisticated.

OLIVER

Rae transferred her dough to her pie plate. She trimmed around the edge, leaving an even inch of overlap. She'd use that later and fold it over the top crust. She was just about to add the filling, when she remembered the dulce de leche. Just like Chef Nancy had warned, it was getting thicker. From now on she'd have to stir it more often. A minute later, she was back to the pie.

RAE

I was only nervous about this challenge for about two minutes. I'm really good at design stuff and I love crafts. Working with dough is almost like working with clay, so I know I'll be able to make a design that will impress the judges.

Chef Nancy held up her hand. "Fifteen minutes!"

Caroline rolled out her dough and picked up a paring knife. She carefully cut out a leaf—one down, thirty to go.

As soon as Chef Nancy said "family," I thought of a family tree, and then I thought about leaves. My pattern is going to be leaves fanning out from the middle of the pie, and in the middle two leaves will come together to form a heart, because family is love.

CAROLINE

"Five minutes!" announced Chef Nancy.

"Aaaaah!" This time it was Caroline protesting. Her leaves were sticking to the table. The butter was melting and making the dough sticky.

The last minutes were busy and silent. Oliver crimped the edges of his crust together with a fork, Rae finished the braided edging of her crust, and Caroline placed two leaves in the center of her pie.

"TIME!" called Chef Nancy.

CHAPTER 18

Caroline, Oliver, and Rae stood at the front of the room, waiting. Their pies all in a row on the big table.

"Our special judge will be here in a minute," promised Chef Nancy.

"Who is it?" whispered Rae.

"Chef Aimee," guessed Caroline. "She's the dessert expert."

Suddenly the door opened and Chef Porter walked in. She stepped up to the table, glanced at the pies, then studied the contestants. "Shall we start?"

"Absolutely," said Chef Nancy. "Oliver, can you explain your design?"

"Yes, ma'am. I wanted a sophisticated design that conveyed the complexity and comfort of family. I chose a latticework pattern because it is woven back and forth like a nest, and the circular pattern in the very center of the pie represents hope."

Rae took a second look at Oliver's pie. It was a simple latticework with a spiral in the center. What was he talking about? Whatever it was, Chef Porter seemed to like it, because she nodded like she agreed.

Next it was Caroline's turn.

"Family made me think of a family tree, which made me think of leaves . . . and love." Caroline pointed to the heart in the middle of her pie.

"Lovely!" said Chef Porter. "Very sweet."

Caroline grinned—nice words from Chef Porter had power.

Chef Nancy turned to Rae. "Rae, tell us about your design?"

"I created a honeycomb design and added a decorative pastry braiding around the edge, because being in a family means working together. There are three people in my family—me, my dad, and my grandmother—and with three strings you can make a braid that is stronger than just one string alone."

Chef Porter quietly studied the pie. "Exquisite!" She stepped back. "Impressive design work, all of you."

Chef Nancy and Chef Porter moved away from the table to discuss the competition.

Minutes later, Chef Porter returned, smiling. "Congratulations, Rae—you are the winner of this challenge. Your pie is absolutely stunning, and the explanation of your inspiration was touching. I don't know what this pie is going to taste like, but it would be a shame to cut into this beautiful crust."

"Thank you, Chef." Rae blushed.

Chef Nancy pointed to the Gadget Wall, then picked up the black board to add a star under Rae's name. Rae watched. Her first star! She was back in the race.

Chef Nancy smiled and pointed again. "Rae, you may pick out your prize."

Chef Porter was gone when Rae came back from the Gadget Wall. Caroline offered a semi-smile and Oliver ignored her. Rae set the mezzaluna on her table. It had a sharp semicircular blade and two wooden handles. Now she'd be a master chopper like Tate. She sighed, put in her toolbox, and stirred her sauce. For the first time ever, winning did not feel as good as she thought it would.

OLIVER

Design is not cooking. Of course she was going to win—she's a craft person. If we were making pies to taste, that would have been fair. I'm the King of Calm, so I won't get upset about it, but this is a cooking competition—not an art show.

CAROLINE

Those leaves took me forever to cut out. I think my design was harder to make than Rae's. I should have had a better explanation. That braiding part won it for her. So I guess words are important.

RAE

The choices we make in cooking are important. Of course the end result is important too, but food is like a story. It has to have meaning. It's creativity plus science plus emotion. Not everyone understands that. I deserved that win.

....

Chef Nancy gathered the group at the front of the room. "I know it's late and you're all tired, but let's bake those pies so we can donate them to the food pantry. What do you think?"

Caroline, Oliver, and Rae all nodded, but none of them looked happy.

Rae beat an egg, glazed her pie, and placed it in the oven. When it came out, it'd have a golden brown crust. Before returning to the big table, she stirred her sauce a few more times. Maybe the others would forget, and burn their dulce de leche. That would serve them right for being grumpy. She smiled for a few seconds, but then felt guilty. She'd rather enjoy her win—not someone else's loss.

CHAPTER 19

hef Nancy didn't notice the restrained mood around the dinner table. She was too excited about the dulce de leche and was eagerly sharing recipe ideas. Now that the sauce had cooled, they were back in the school studio ready to try it.

Oliver stirred his sauce. The white milky liquid had transformed: it was creamy, thick, and brown—maybe too brown. He pulled out a saucepan lid, ready to cover it up, if anyone came close.

The rich, sweet smell filled Caroline's nose and she closed her eyes.

Chef Nancy scanned the room. "You may taste it, but only one spoonful each. We'll save the rest for tomorrow."

"OH MY GOSH!" Rae's hand fluttered in the air. "It's SOOOO good!"

"De . . . li . . . cious!" murmered Caroline.

"Mmmmm mmmm mmmmm!" Oliver choked down a

spoonful. His dulce de leche was definitely burnt. He covered the pot.

Chef Nancy held up a roll of plastic wrap. "It's getting late. Let's wrap it up."

RAE

> Dulce de leche is amazing. I want to put it on everything and I want to cook with it. It's like finding a whole new ingredient that you didn't even know existed. As soon as I get home I'm going to make some. My grandma is going to love it.

····

It was lights out when they got back to the lodge. Chef Nancy pointed at Rae. "And no chit-chatting. Tomorrow's a really *big* day. I want you all well rested."

Rae collapsed on her bed. "UGH!" What a tiring day. She didn't want to think about it, any of it—the good or the bad.

Caroline pulled her pillow into her arms. "Your honeycomb pie design was *really* good."

Rae looked up surprised. "Aw, thank you!" She paused. "Are you worried about Oliver? You both have two stars."

"I've been so focused on my own cooking, I haven't had time to worry." Caroline yawned and pulled up the covers.

Rae sat up. "Maybe we should do that visualization thing too!"

Caroline closed her eyes. "Okay, I'm walking up to my food truck, Diner Française, and I see … Wait! It's you!" Caroline waved her arm. "And you're walking up to your food truck, the Crafty Café."

Rae leaned back on her pillow. "You're right! We both have food trucks!" She waved back to Caroline. If it was pretend, it might as well be perfect.

CHAPTER 20

C hef Nancy greeted everyone with the same four words. "Big day! Get ready!" The pattern at the breakfast table was the same as always: eat fast and listen.

Chef Nancy shared the schedule for the day. "We'll start with a visit to the Flower Meadow. That's a designated space here on the farm, available for special events. Then we'll come back to the filming studio for interviews and to start the challenge. And finally, we'll head back to the Flower Meadow to finish up."

Chef Nancy pointed to the door. "We'll leave in twenty minutes."

Thirty minutes later, the golf cart was winding through an unfamiliar part of the estate.

Chef Nancy pointed to a white tent in the distance. "That's the Flower Meadow tent."

Caroline felt a twinge in her stomach. This was her chance to beat Oliver, and then if she won again, maybe even hold the Golden Envelope.

As they got closer, the tent got larger and larger until it was clearly the biggest and most spectacular tent any of them had ever seen.

"It's like a mansion!" gasped Rae.

Chef Nancy led the way in. They passed through a giant ballroom: wood floor, multiple chandeliers, and flowers everywhere.

"It must be a wedding!" whispered Caroline.

Chef Gary, Chef Aimee, Chef Porter, and the cameras were waiting in the next room. It was smaller than the first, and the ceiling was covered with tiny fairy lights.

Caroline twirled in a circle, looking up. "It's magical!"

"Ballerina?" asked Chef Porter. Caroline froze. Chef Porter smiled. "Don't worry, I like your compliment." She turned back to the group. "Welcome, everyone, to Flower Meadow."

Chef Aimee moved next to Chef Porter. "Who knows what a *quinceañera* is?"

"A fruit?" asked Caroline.

Chef Aimee shook her head. "Quince is a fruit, but a *quinceañera* is a celebration. It's a Latin American tradition celebrating a girl's fifteenth birthday."

Chef Aimee gestured toward the ballroom. "It's a big party with dancing, fancy clothes, speeches, and, of course, a

lot of food. Our *quinceañera* today is Olivia, and she and her parents, and four special friends, will be the judges for today's challenge."

Caroline shot a look at Rae. The judges weren't going to judge?

Just then, the door behind Chef Gary opened and two people walked into the room.

Chef Gary motioned them forward. "Welcome, Mrs. Rios. Welcome, Olivia. I'd like you to meet our talented young chefs." He introduced everyone, then continued: "Today's challenge is to prepare two desserts, one traditional and one inventive. The traditional dessert is called *alfajores,* a sandwich cookie filled with dulce de leche."

"Dulce de leche!" whispered Rae. "So that's why we made it."

Mrs. Rios reached into her purse and pulled out a sheet of paper. "I brought you my grandmother's recipe."

Chef Porter took the recipe. "Thank you, Mrs. Rios. What a special honor for our young chefs. I am sure they will not disappoint."

Chef Gary moved next to Olivia. "I understand you have a favorite sweet treat that you'd like to see incorporated into a dessert. Is that correct?"

Olivia nodded. "It's my favorite thing ever—cotton candy! It fun to eat and tastes great! What's not to like?" She grinned.

"Cotton candy!" repeated Chef Gary. "This is will be the feature in your second dessert." Chef Gary looked down the line of young chefs. Are you ready for this challenge?"

"YES, CHEF!"

"Me too," agreed Chef Aimee. "I can't wait to see what you make."

"CUT!" yelled Steve.

Chef Nancy gathered the young chefs together and led them back outside to the golf cart.

Caroline smiled all the way back to the filming studio. Desserts! This was her specialty. She could win this!

CHAPTER 21

CAROLINE

I'm not scared of this challenge. I'm like Olivia—I like cotton candy. I won't go for something subtle. If you like cotton candy, you want a one hundred percent cotton candy flavor overload.

I don't think the cookies will be hard to make. Olivia wants cotton candy and my twist is to give her that flavor mixed with a new texture. Cotton candy melts in your mouth and then it's gone. I'm going to make something that's more substantial, something that lasts.

OLIVER

RAE

I was watching Olivia. She seems bubbly and fun. I bet she'd like a whimsical dessert, something that looks special . . . and tastes great, of course. I'm still thinking, but I have some ideas.

••••

After the interviews, everyone lined up behind the big table, facing the judges.

"ROLLING!"

Chef Gary tapped the top of his head. "Is this full of ideas?"

"Yes, Chef!"

He smiled. "And I bet you can't wait to get started."

"YES, CHEF!"

Chef Aimee stepped forward with a green bag.

Oliver groaned.

Chef Aimee shook the bag. "That's right. Team challenge with two teams!"

Rae looked at Caroline, then Oliver. Team challenge? But how? There were only three of them.

Chef Aimee called Rae to the front and presented her with the bag. "Please pick out the name of your teammate."

Rae pulled out an envelope and handed it to Chef Aimee.

Chef Aimee opened it, then smiled. "Mystery!" She held out the card: it was blank except for a giant question mark.

She turned to Caroline. "This means you and Oliver will be partners."

Rae looked around frantically. Two against one? That wasn't fair.

Chef Gary chuckled. "Rae, you look worried. No need—we've brought in a special guest to help you."

Rae's palms were sweaty. Her heart was racing. It was hard to cook with someone you knew and trusted, but cooking with a stranger? This was going to be even more of a disadvantage.

Chef Gary pointed toward the back of the room. "And here comes your partner!"

Rae inhaled a fast breath, then turned around. "TA-AATE!"

Tate raced down the ramp, high-fived Oliver and Caroline, and jumped right next to Rae. She gave him a big hug.

Chef Gary gave everyone a minute to calm down. "Welcome back, Tate. It's great to have you here to help with the team challenge." He clapped his hands. "Okay, let's get serious. This is not going to be easy. You have a lot to do, in a limited time. You'll need to create two dessert items: traditional *alfajores* using your own dulce de leche, and a creative dessert featuring cotton candy." Chef Gary held up his hand. "But, unlike the other challenges of this past week, we need you to provide us with not one, but eight samples of each. You have two hours to complete this challenge." He studied each of the young chefs. "Can you do it?"

"YES, CHEF!" The answer was thunderous.

Chef Aimee covered her ears. "That's what we like to hear. We'll have a cotton candy machine available for you to use, as well as cotton candy flavoring and sugars in the pantry. You'll have ten minutes to discuss your ideas and create a pantry list." She raised her hand. "And that time starts . . . NOW!"

"My station!" yelled Oliver.

"My station!" shouted Rae.

"DUH!" shouted Tate. "I don't have a station." It was ten minutes filled with loud talking, frantic note-taking, and compromise.

There are good things and not so good things about having Oliver as a partner. He's a great cook, so that part is a bonus, but he really likes getting things his own way. He loved my idea for mini cheesecakes, but now he's added cookie cups. That's more work, but like he says, you can't win this without innovation. Teamwork is compromise.

CAROLINE

RAE

Caroline and Oliver have two dulce de leches to choose from. Not that it matters, though, because mine turned out great. I'm mostly excited about the cotton candy challenge. We're making mini cotton candy milkshakes and decorating them with candy and cotton candy cookies. Tate has creative ideas and we work well together. I'm lucky to have him as a partner.

> Caroline is a strong partner and we work well as a team. I don't have any doubts about her cooking ability. That's important, because it means I don't have to double-check what she's doing. Making mini cheese-cakes was a good idea, but adding the cookie cups makes it a great idea.

OLIVER

"Two more minutes!" said Chef Gary.

Rae scribbled down some last-minute ingredients, Oliver went over his list, Caroline looked at Mrs. Rios's recipe, and Tate did some jumping jacks.

TATE

> When we do the pantry run, Rae will grab the big stuff and I'll grab the little things. I'm fast, so we're being smart about using my strengths. I'm glad I could come back to help her.

CHAPTER 22

G O!" shouted Chef Aimee, and everyone took off for the pantry. Rae made two trips back to her workstation to drop off supplies. This time there would be no going back.

"Don't forget the sprinkles!" shouted Rae.

Tate spun around and headed back to the shelf.

"Sprinkles!" repeated Caroline. She followed Tate. She'd forgotten them too.

"TIME!" called Chef Aimee.

"CUT!" yelled Steve.

Chef Nancy waved her arms. "Leave your baskets at your workstations and come back to the pantry." She rolled a cotton candy machine to the center of the space.

"We want everyone to have the same opportunity for success, so here are a few last-minute instructions. First, once you've made your pastry for the *alfajores*, put it in the refrigerator for at least an hour. This is part of Mrs. Rios's recipe. Do not ignore this step. Second, I want to show you how to use the cotton candy machine. We have pink sugar and blue sugar."

Chef Nancy gave a quick demonstration of the machine. "Any questions?"

Four heads shook simultaneously.

"I can't wait to try it!" whispered Caroline.

"We'll see," said Oliver.

Caroline scowled. What did that mean?

Five minutes later the teams were back at their workstations, waiting for the official start.

Chef Gary raised his hands: "LET'S GET COOKING!"

Rae and Tate had a plan: first the *alfajores* cookie dough, so it could go into the fridge; then the ice cream, so it could set in the freezer; and last the cotton candy pinwheel cookies.

Rae mixed the cornstarch, flour, baking powder, baking soda, and salt in a bowl. Tate creamed the butter and sugar in the mixer, then carefully added the egg yolks one at a time before adding the vanilla.

"We have to be careful when we add the flour," warned Rae. "If we overmix it, the cookies will be tough."

Caroline got to the fridge with their *alfajores* dough just seconds before Tate. She rushed back to work on her cheesecake.

"Crust into oven," barked Oliver.

"On it!" Caroline held up a rectangular glass baking dish. There wasn't time for full sentences.

Chef Aimee walked up just as Caroline was pressing the graham crust into the dish. "What are you making?"

"Cheesecake. Oliver thought it would cook faster if it was spread out, and since we're cutting it up to serve it . . ."

"It doesn't make a difference," interrupted Oliver. "So faster is better."

"What's next?" asked Chef Aimee.

"Sugar cones!" answered Caroline.

"Cheesecake mixture!" insisted Oliver.

"Hmm." Chef Aimee looked back and forth between the two of them. "Seems like you two might need to get on the same page." She turned and left them staring at each other.

Getting on the same page involved lots of whispering.

"What makes you the boss?" snapped Caroline.

Oliver looked around, then lowered his voice. "We don't have time for this, so I'll just tell you. I've had lessons and training. I know what I'm doing! I'm not some homeschooled wannabe chef!"

Caroline stepped back eyes wide. "You had lessons? From professionals?"

Oliver brushed it off. "So what? Like you didn't?"

Caroline shook her head.

"Really?" Oliver smirked. "Your mom, the chef. She's not a professional? Get over it, Caroline. You're just like me!"

••••

"What are you making?" Chef Porter rested her hands on the counter.

Tate looked up, surprised. He hadn't seen her coming.

"Uh . . ." Chef Porter always made him nervous.

"Cotton candy ice cream," answered Rae. She held up her spoon, then quickly put it back in the saucepan and stirred. "I'm mixing milk, whipping cream, sugar, salt, egg yolks, vanilla, and cotton candy syrup. I can't stop stirring or it'll burn."

"Yes, of course." Chef Porter turned back to Tate. "And what are you making?"

Tate didn't look up. He fumbled with the stand mixer and mumbled something about being busy.

"Busy doing what?" asked Chef Porter. Now she was scowling.

Tate dropped a stick of butter into the mixing bowl and turned it on high. Rae watched. This was not going well. Tate had nothing to lose—he didn't have to be nice. Rae pulled her saucepan off the heat, grabbed a measuring cup, and stepped in front of Tate. She smiled at Chef Porter. "Excuse me, Chef Porter, I just need to reach the sugar."

"Oh, certainly." Chef Porter stepped back.

Rae measured out half a cup of sugar and added it to Tate's butter mixture. "Tate, can you measure out the dry ingredients, over there?" Rae pointed to the far end of the counter.

Tate nodded, more than happy to escape Chef Porter.

"We're making cotton candy pinwheel cookies with pink and blue swirls," explained Rae. She cracked an egg and added it to the bowl.

"I'll come back later," said Chef Porter. "I'd like to see how you put those together."

As soon as Chef Porter was gone, Tate was back with the flour mixture and an apology.

Rae nodded. "Next time she comes over, just let me do the talking."

Twenty minutes later, when the judges were making rounds, it was Chef Aimee, not Chef Porter, who stopped by.

Tate rolled a ball of blue dough into a nine-inch flat square, then brushed it with water and covered it with a pink square of dough the same size. He gently push the two doughs together with a rolling pin.

Rae brushed the top of the pink square with water. "This is the fun part." Starting from one edge, she carefully rolled the dough over on itself until she had a chubby tube-shaped log.

Tate brushed the log with water and rolled it in sprinkles. "Now it goes in the freezer to harden, then we'll slice it into cookies and bake them."

"Impressive teamwork!" said Chef Aimee. "I'm excited to see how this all comes together."

"Me too." Tate waved and ran off to the freezer.

CHAPTER 23

"SIXTY MINUTES!"

Caroline looked up at the clock, then down at the oven. "Sixty minutes? I don't think it's even close to being cooked! Can you tell? Can you?"

Oliver bent down to look. He was worried too. "It's close—ten minutes, maybe fifteen."

Caroline marched back and forth between the oven and the worktable.

Oliver watched. "That pacing's not going to help. Let's work on the *alfajores*. You get the dough from the fridge and I'll prepare the baking sheets with parchment paper."

When Caroline came back, Oliver rolled out the dough, and then he and Caroline stamped out twenty-two circles, enough for eleven finished cookies.

Caroline picked up the leftover dough. "Should we do more? Just in case."

Oliver studied the baking trays. "Fine, if you can fit them in. But there isn't time for another whole tray."

Caroline nodded and stamped out seven more circles. She placed them on the baking sheets. When Oliver pulled out the cheesecake, she was ready with the cookies.

"Twelve minutes," said Oliver

Caroline set the timer. "Should we use my dulce de leche or yours?"

Oliver paused. "Let's use yours—I want you to feel good about this challenge."

"Really? Okay." Caroline ran off the fridge, smiling. Oliver really was a team player!

••••

"FORTY MINUTES!"

Rae pulled out three trays from the oven.

Tate held up a dark brown cookie. "Oh no."

"This one too!" Rae tossed it to the side.

Chef Gary arrived just as Tate was doing a cookie count. "Thirty-three perfect ones for *alafores*! It's good we made extras."

"What's next?" asked Chef Gary.

"More cookies, pinwheels." Tate ran to the freezer to get the dough.

While he was gone, Rae stirred the dulce de leche. It was room temperature and perfectly spreadable. She lifted the spoon, sniffed it, then put it back down.

Chef Gary laughed. "It's hard not to lick that, isn't it?"

Rae nodded. "I didn't know it before, but dulce de leche is *heaven!*"

Tate set the pinwheel cookie log on the table. "Who gets to cut it?"

Rae handed him a knife. "Master Chopper."

Three minutes later, eighteen perfect pinwheel circles were laying on the baking sheet.

Chef Gary tapped the table. "Nice job, you two."

Tate put the baking sheet into the oven while Chef Gary moved to the center of the room. "TWENTY-FIVE MINUTES!"

....

Rae and Tate were right on schedule. There wasn't time to rest, but they weren't in a panic. They worked together on the *alfajores,* spreading the dulce de leche and then rolling the edges of the cookie in coconut.

"It's good we had extras," said Tate. He pushed a broken wafer to the side. "They sure break easy—they're so crumbly."

Caroline and Oliver were not so fortunate.

"Do you think they'll notice?" whispered Caroline. "We should have turned the baking pans around."

Oliver quickly covered the brown edges of the cookie with a generous scoop of dulce de leche. "We'll roll them in extra coconut. No one will know. The dulce de leche is all they can taste."

Caroline nodded, looked around, then stopped. It was overwhelming. There was so much to do! They still had to make cotton candy, cotton candy whipped cream, *and* the sugar cone cups. She leaned on the counter with her head in her hands. It was too much!

Oliver rushed over. "What are you doing?" Caroline didn't move. He tried again. "Go make the cotton candy. You wanted to do it. GO! I'll do the cookie cups."

Caroline straightened up, glared at Oliver, and stomped over to the cotton candy machine.

Oliver shook his head. They were in trouble. There was no way he could finish this alone. He dropped a spoonful of cookie batter onto the parchment paper and swirled it into a perfect circle. In ten minutes these would be baked, and Caroline *had* to be back to help shape them.

Cotton candy is magical. It looks like a cloud, but it's more than that. It really has powers. Making the cotton candy changed everything for me. I don't know if it was the color, or the smell, or the fluffiness, but it really made me feel hopeful!

CAROLINE

"TEN MINUTES!"

"Last five cookie cups!" said Oliver. He pulled the tray out of the oven, and then he and Caroline peeled off the parchment paper, and quickly shaped the cookies over upside-down ramekins. Once they were cool, they'd be ready to use.

OLIVER

We're going to fill the sugar cookie cups with scoops of cotton candy cheesecake, then add cotton candy whipped cream and top the whole thing off with sprinkles and pink cotton candy. It'll look festive, and taste delicious. It's a winning combination.

Putting the ice cream milkshakes together was my favorite part. We put frosting on the rim of the glasses to hold the cotton candy in place, then filled them with the milkshake mixture and added cotton candy whipped cream and sprinkles. And last but not least, we added the pinwheel cookie and a straw.

RAE

"TIME!"

Caroline put her hands in the air. A second later, they fell heavily against her sides. She was exhausted.

CHAPTER 24

The judges walked back and forth between the workstations.

Chef Aimee pointed to the milkshakes. "Festive and colorful!"

Chef Gary admired the cookie cups. "Inventive and useful."

Chef Porter studied the *alfajores*. "Classic and sophisticated."

Oliver, Rae, Caroline, and Tate stood watching, too tired to talk. When the judges were done, they stood in front of the young chefs and applauded—even Chef Porter.

Chef helpers came in to pack and transport the desserts to the Flower Meadow tent for the judging. Caroline watched them go. She sighed as the door closed. "This is the hard part—waiting!"

Tate grabbed a juice box. "Well, I don't mind it. I'm happy I'm here."

"Me too!" said Oliver, and he tossed him an orange.

Playing catch was their thing. Tate smiled and threw it back.

····

An hour later everyone was back in the golf cart.

The judges and cameras were waiting in the second room, just like last time, but this time Olivia, her parents, and the special friends—four boys and four girls—were there too.

Chef Gary motioned the chefs forward. "Welcome back!" He introduced the young chefs, then turned to Chef Aimee.

She waved a stack of cards. "We have the results. This was a tightly fought competition, and there were some great comments. We'll start with the cotton candy dessert."

Chef Aimee pointed to Oliver and Caroline. "Your cheesecake dessert was a big home run in the taste department: *delicious, tongue-candy, drool-worthy, yummy, excellent, fantastic-licious*—these are just some of the comments. However, not everyone was excited about the cookie cup. There were some concerns about it crumbling and being messy."

Chef Aimee pointed at Rae and Tate. "Wow! Those milkshakes got a lot of smiles. Visually, it was the clear winner: *Wonderful, best-brain-freeze, outstanding, scrumptious, delectable, glamtastic*—very good comments. However, a number of people thought it might be too sweet."

Chef Porter put an arm around Mrs. Rios and patted her shoulder. "Mrs. Rios was very generous with us and shared her family's recipe for *alfajores*. The winning team will be responsible for the *alfajores* served at the party. This continues a tradition started many generations ago. It is a great honor. I have asked Mrs. Rios to introduce the winning team."

Mrs. Rios coughed nervously. She put her fingers to her lips and made a kissing sound.

Rae stifled a giggle.

"The dulce de leche was delicious! The wafer cookies were delicate. My heart is happy. Thank you, Rae and Tate, for making my abuela's *alfajores*!"

Rae and Tate grinned, but who was the BIG winner?

Chef Gary stepped to the front. He thanked Mr. and Mrs. Rios, Olivia, and all her friends.

Caroline felt hot, too hot. She wiped her forehead with her sleeve. This waiting was torture. She shifted uncomfortably.

"Caroline and Oliver, your cotton candy dessert was delicious, but hard to eat. There were a few standout *alfajores* in your collection, but unfortunately they were standing out for the wrong reason."

Oliver stared at the ground.

Caroline turned a bright shade of red.

Chef Gary frowned. "We've covered this before. When something is less than perfect, we leave it *off* the plate—we don't try to hide it."

Chef Porter turned to Rae and Tate and smiled. "You made us proud. Congratulations, Rae and Tate. You are the winners of this challenge."

"THANK YOU, CHEF!" And then Tate smiled right back at Chef Porter.

"Now it's two stars each," whispered Tate. "Anyone could win that Golden Envelope."

Rae nodded. It was like starting fresh, like back at the beginning. They all had the same chance.

CHAPTER 25

fter lunch, Rae and Tate left to manage the making and baking of their winning desserts. Oliver and Caroline stayed in the lodge, silent and brooding. Caroline would be called later for her photo shoot for *Creative Cooking.*

"This way," said Chef Nancy, and she pointed to the Porter restaurant kitchen.

Rae was worried. "Do you think we can do it?"

"Of course. These are professional chefs. Think of them as your hands. You and Tate are there to help them. To make sure the hands are doing what they need to do." She smiled. "It's a good experience. In fact, you might really enjoy it."

Chef Nancy was right—it was fun. And Rae and Tate felt like celebrities.

"Do you think this is how Chef Gary feels?" asked Rae.

Tate nodded. "And Chef Aimee, too."

Six professional chefs meant twelve hands to manage, but it wasn't hard. The chefs had Mrs. Rios's recipe, Rae's dulce de leche, and Rae and Tate to answer their questions. *Yes, the dough should be crumbly. Pull the cookies out before they get golden brown. One fast roll in the coconut is best.* And when it was time to make the cotton candy milkshake, Tate and Rae put one together for the chefs to copy.

There was even time for a photo—Tate and Rae standing in the middle of the helper chefs, surrounded by their desserts.

••••

Chef Nancy arrived five minutes later. "So? How was it?"

"I want my own kitchen," said Tate. "I want to be the boss . . . every day."

Rae wasn't so sure. "I liked it, but I don't really want to be a boss. I like it when it's smaller. Maybe two people working together, like in a food truck."

Chef Nancy nodded. "That's what experiences are for. So you can decide what's good for you."

••••

When they got to the lodge, Rae ran straight to Caroline. "How was the photo shoot? Did you feel like a superstar?"

"Uncomfortable!" complained Caroline. "I don't like standing completely still in one place for thirty minutes. I'm glad I'm not a model."

Rae laughed and hugged her friend.

Oliver and Tate were playing catch with a Bosc pear.

When it was time to leave, Tate waved all the way to the door. "Good luck! Good choices! Good cooking!"

Rae ran over to give him an extra hug. "Thank you."

And then, once again, it was just the three of them.

CHAPTER 26

C hef Nancy arrived at the breakfast table with a happy "Good morning." "The sun is shining and I'm excited! Today's excursion is a farmer's market . . . and not just any farmer's market, but the biggest one in this region."

"Tower Market?" asked Rae.

"Exactly," said Chef Nancy. "You've heard of it?"

"Oh my gosh!" Caroline pushed her chair away and stood up. "I've always wanted to go there. It's the place where they throw the fish."

Oliver sat up, suddenly interested. "Hey, I've seen that place on TV. Do we get to catch fish?"

Chef Nancy raised her hands. "We won't know until we get there."

Oliver grinned. "That sounds like a yes."

••••

Forty minutes after leaving, they arrived at the Tower Market gates.

"We have a special pass," said Chef Nancy. "We can park right in front." Mark and Janet the camerapeople were waiting, and Steve the producer watched from off to the side.

The market was noisy, busy, and exciting. There were food stalls everywhere, and people rushed by with bags filled with flowers, fresh produce, meat and cheeses, and anything else you could imagine.

Chef Nancy pointed to an aisle on the left. "This way to our first stop."

Rae found it hard to keep up. There was so much to look at. There wasn't just food at the market—there were crafts, too! Chef Nancy finally stopped in front of a cheese shop. A lady in an apron was standing out front, waiting for them.

Chef Nancy shook her hand. "This is Miss Catherine,

otherwise known as Catherine Woods. She's an accomplished cheesemaker and one of the proprietors of Woods Hole Cheese."

"Thank you, Chef, and welcome to my stall. My family has been selling cheese at this market for over seventy years. We have our own dairy and make all our cheeses on our farm. We sell cow, goat, and buffalo cheeses. Who here has ever tried to milk a water buffalo?"

Nobody raised a hand.

Miss Catherine chuckled. "Well, it's not easy, because they are very temperamental animals." She raised a finger. "But it's worth it. I've brought out some samples for you to taste." She held out a wooden board with two mounds of cheese. "See if you can tell the difference between cow mozzarella and buffalo mozzarella."

Oliver raised his hand. "The buffalo mozzarella is creamier and richer. Does it have a higher fat content?"

"Exactly!" gushed Miss Catherine. "Wow! Well done, young man."

Rae frowned. Oliver was always showing off.

Miss Catherine offered another board of cheeses. There was an aged cheddar, a smoked Gouda, and a Gruyère.

Caroline raised her hand. "Gruyère is like Swiss cheese, but tangy and better."

Miss Catherine nodded. "Well, certainly compared to the processed Swiss cheese you find in the grocery store. Gruyère is actually named after a village in Switzerland."

"I like the cheddar," said Rae. "It's bitey!"

Miss Catherine laughed. "I've never heard it described that way, but it's true. It does have a little sharpness to it."

"Thank you," said Chef Nancy, "for sharing your family's passion with us."

Everyone clapped.

Chef Nancy raised her hand. "Next stop. Follow me."

"What's next?" asked Rae.

Chef Nancy shook her head and kept walking.

"Fish!" said Oliver. "I bet it's fish!"

After a few more twists and turns down the crowded aisles, they stopped. "LOOK!" shouted Caroline. She tugged on Rae's arm. "It's Beckner's Fish Market!"

"I'm first," announced Oliver.

Rae shrugged—she wasn't going to fight him on this one. She wasn't sure she even wanted to catch a fish.

Chef Nancy waved at a man behind the counter. He waved back and walked out to meet them.

"Caroline, Rae, and Oliver, this is Jim. His family has operated this fish stall since 1946."

"Who likes fish?" asked Jim.

All hands went up.

"And shrimp?"

The hands stayed up.

"Well, let's try some samples!"

There was fresh shrimp, sautéed octopus, seared tuna, and even salmon jerky, and all of it was delicious.

Oliver raised his hand. "Are we going to catch the fish? Like on TV?"

"Now?" asked Jim.

"YES!" Caroline bounced up and down. "But I only want to catch a little one? Something like a tilapia or a fresh water trout?"

"Whoa! These kids know their fish." Jim picked a trout out of the case and put it on the counter. He gave Caroline a piece of paper and showed her how to hold her hands. "It's not like catching a football. It's more like catching a baby. You have to kind of cradle it. And the paper will help you grip it. These fish are slippery."

A crowd was gathering to watch. Rae was glad she wasn't

first. Jim positioned Caroline across the aisle then moved back to the fish counter. "Are you ready?"

Caroline raised her hand. A second later a fish was flying across the aisle.

"HUZZA!" cheered the crowd. Caroline had caught it.

Oliver was next, and then Rae.

RAE

I dropped my fish. I don't know how Caroline was able to hold on to hers. It was so slippery. Oliver caught his, and of course it was bigger than ours. My poor little tilapia. I felt bad when it hit the pavement.

After the fish-catching, Chef Nancy led the group back behind Jim's stall. There was a long table set up with three cutting boards, three knives, and three fish. "How about a challenge?" asked Jim.

Rae groaned.

Oliver smiled and took an apron from Chef Nancy. Those restaurant lessons were about to pay off. "Thank you, ma'am."

CHAPTER 27

Jim moved to the head of the table. "We're going to do this together. I'm going to show you how to fillet and debone a trout." He held up his knife. "A good sharp filleting knife is the only tool you'll need."

"And this isn't a race," warned Chef Nancy. "We are only looking for the cleanest fillet. That will be the winner."

Rae followed along but it wasn't easy. There was a trick to the knife. It had a flexible blade and you had to keep it pressed against the table while cutting.

I know it wasn't a race, but I finished first. I know how to clean, fillet, debone, and skin a fish. My fillet was the cleanest—not one single bone, and the skin was free from flesh. You have to respect talent.

OLIVER

"Only three bones!" said Caroline. "And it was my first time. I bet I could get good at that."

Rae shook her head. "Not me. I totally messed up—nine bones! And worse, now Oliver's in the lead with the most stars!"

Caroline shrugged. "Don't give up, you never know. Chef Nancy's full of surprises."

....

After a lunch stop for ramen noodles, they were back exploring the market. Chef Nancy pointed out interesting produce, a pickle-maker, a hot sauce store, and a Chinese bakery, but they did not stop for another challenge.

"We're here!" announced Chef Nancy. "Our last stop!"

Rae looked up and read the sign. "The Mushroom Man?"

Chef Nancy nodded. "Don is truly *the* Mushroom Man. He knows everything about mushrooms and sells some wonderful varieties."

CAROLINE

Oliver must have eaten too much seafood, or too much ramen. He said he didn't feel well and couldn't try any of the mushrooms. Chef Nancy was pretty worried. We tried five different kinds: enoki, oyster, shiitake, chanterelles, and morels. Morels were my favorite. They are meaty and savory and don't taste anything like a regular mushroom.

"Can I have yours?" Rae pointed to Oliver's plate.

He nodded and held his stomach.

Rae scooped up a mouthful of morels. "These are amazing!"

Caroline agreed. "And mushrooms aren't even my favorites."

Oliver felt a stab of regret. Should he have tried them? Forced himself? No, too risky. Great chefs were supposed to love all ingredients. It was a risk to let anyone see his weakness—he couldn't stand mushrooms.

Chef Nancy stepped forward. "We have one more mini-challenge." She looked at Oliver. "Are you up for it?"

"Yes, ma'am."

"Don has been gracious enough to set up an unusual challenge—mushroom related, of course."

Oliver scowled.

"Now that you've tried some of the varieties, we're going to test your knowledge. You'll each have five different mushrooms and five recipes . . . that are missing their mushrooms. Place your mushroom on top of the appropriate recipe card. The first one to pair all their mushrooms with the correct recipes wins."

Oliver grinned. Just because he didn't like them didn't mean he wasn't knowledgeable. He could do this.

Chef Nancy passed out the recipe cards and gave each contestant a bag of mushrooms. You may start . . . NOW!"

Rae dumped her mushrooms out onto the table. She had portabella, enoki, shiitake, morel, and porcini mushrooms.

Now for the recipes. The portabella was the easiest to find. Stuffed Mushroom Cap—that had to be it. Shiitake had to be Asian Cabbage Stir Fry. Only three left.

"DONE!" Oliver raised his hands.

Chef Nancy rushed over to check his choices. "Congratulations, Oliver—you win!"

"AH!" Caroline dropped her cards on the table.

Rae felt exactly the same.

••••

Chef Nancy bought old-fashioned candy sticks for the ride home. Everyone had one, even Oliver. He smiled. "I suddenly feel a lot better."

Rae knew why—the Golden Envelope! Tomorrow, Oliver would have the advantage.

When they got back, Chef Nancy sent Oliver over to the Gadget Wall to pick out his prizes. While he was gone, Chef Nancy pulled out the big black board. Rae and Caroline watched her add two stars under Oliver's name.

"Mini-grinder and mezzaluna!" Oliver swaggered back, holding his prizes in the air.

Caroline and Rae both nodded. The STP meant being supportive, no matter what. Rae did her best not to grumble. Not always so easy to do.

Chef Nancy made an official presentation of the Golden Envelope. Oliver wasn't allowed to look inside until tomorrow at the elimination challenge, but Chef Nancy let him hold it, just for a minute.

That night, Oliver fell asleep smiling. Optimism was not the feeling across the hall.

Rae flopped onto her bed. "Why even try? Oliver has the advantage."

Caroline pushed her face into her pillow, then sat up.

Rae moved next to her. "We have to beat him, but it won't be easy—he's like a genius or something."

Caroline shook her head.

"Yes, we can do it. Together!"

Caroline shook her head again. "No, not that. He's not a genius!" And then she confessed what she knew about the cooking lessons he had taken before the competition.

Rae was mad! Mad at Caroline—*I can't believe you didn't tell me!* But mostly she was mad at Oliver. *Really? He called me that? A homeschooled wannabe chef!*

It was the exact fuel she needed to be fired up for the next day.

"I'm sorry," cried Caroline.

Rae nodded. There was nothing else to say.

CHAPTER 28

Caroline, Oliver, and Rae were quiet at breakfast. Chef Nancy filled up the silence. She talked about the weather and the visit to Tower Market. No one spoke about the enormity of the day. Steve came in to check on things while they were eating, but Chef Nancy waved him away.

When breakfast was done, she pushed her chair back and stood up. "I won't pretend that today isn't important. Today's challenge is huge, and I want you to do your best. Remember, it's not over until it's over. Think about what you've learned over these last two weeks, and apply that knowledge. You are better cooks today than you were a week ago and I am proud of each and every one of you." Chef Nancy looked them each in the eye.

"Interviews!" It was Steve.

Chef Nancy nodded. "Right, two minutes!" She looked back at the table. "Ready?"

Everyone stood up. "YES, CHEF!"

CAROLINE

I am going to win today's competition because . . . I need to win. I have skills and knowledge, but I also have my own creativity, and that is something that is all me. This is a chance to prove myself.

Of course I'm going to win. That's what I came here for. No matter what, I'm up for the challenge. I think I've proven myself this week. I don't know what kind of advantage the Golden Envelope will give me, but I'm glad to have it.

OLIVER

RAE

I will win today's challenge because I have faith. Faith in what I can do. It's something you can't measure or see or teach, but I feel it. It's that little voice inside saying *Yes, you can,* and that feels powerful.

....

After the interviews, the junior chefs visited their parents for an hour. There were hugs and last-minute advice, and then it was time to line up.

Caroline, Oliver, and Rae stood in a line outside the filming studio door. In just minutes, the announcer would introduce them and it would start. No one said anything.

"ROLLING!" shouted Steve.

"*Next Best Junior Chef* is proud to invite our three junior chefs to the second elimination round of this competition. Please welcome Caroline, Oliver, and Rae."

The door opened and they walked one after another, down the ramp, to the front of the room.

Chef Gary clapped his hands. "What a week! You have really showed your determination and skill, and here we are at another elimination challenge. I think you're ready, more than ready. What do you say?"

"YES, CHEF!"

Rae's heart was racing. Chef Gary was right. She was ready.

"Our junior chefs spent a day at Tower Market, where they met some very interesting people. I would like to invite those people to come forward."

Chef Gary introduced them and they each put a box on the big table. "Miss Catherine is purveyor of Woods Hole Cheese, Jim Beckner is the owner of Beckner's Fish Market, and Don Restero is the Mushroom Man. We have one more addition to our table, and that is from our own Chef Porter." Chef Porter walked forward and added a small box to the table.

Caroline tried to think ahead. It had to be a fish challenge, but with cheese and mushrooms?

Chef Aimee stepped forward with the green bag.

Caroline stifled groan. She hated that bag!

"Oliver, will you please step forward and take an envelope?" She asked the same of Caroline, and then she reached into the bag and handed the last one to Rae. "Please do not open your envelopes until instructed to do so."

Oliver tapped the envelope against his leg. He wanted his Golden Envelope advantage, and then he wanted to get started. All this talking made him fidgety and uneasy—the opposite of calm.

Chef Gary put his arm around Jim. "Jim and I go way back, and I was honored that he agreed to participate in our competition. I understand you all did some fish-catching."

Oliver perked up.

"Well, Jim has brought you each a fish for today's challenge. And surprise, surprise! It's the same kind of fish as the one you caught. Caroline will have lake trout, Oliver will have black cod, and Rae will have tilapia."

Everyone clapped. Rae smiled—tilapia was good. She could work with that.

Chef Porter pointed to the table. "Miss Catherine, Don Restero, and I have also contributed to this challenge. We have each brought you one ingredient to use as the prominent flavor in your fish dish. You may now open your envelope and read out your mystery ingredient."

"Honey," said Caroline.

"Mushrooms," said Oliver.

"Cheese." Rae frowned. Cheese and tilapia? This wasn't going to be easy.

Chef Gary held up the Golden Envelope. He handed it to Oliver. "Oliver, you are the winner of the Golden Envelope and this gives you an advantage in this challenge. You may swap your ingredients with anyone else. Or you can keep the mushrooms and black cod."

"SWAP!" announced Oliver. "With Rae for the tilapia and cheese."

Rae was stunned. Chef Gary was too. "Really?"

"Yes, sir."

Chef Gary stepped back to the center of the room. "You have sixty minutes to prepare your fish and an accompanying side dish. Do you accept this challenge?"

"YES, CHEF!"

"CUT!" yelled Steve.

"WORKSTATIONS!" shouted Chef Nancy. "I'll come by and check in. Caroline, you'll be first."

"It's not easy to think fast," complained Caroline, "but I do have some ideas. Having to use the honey actually helps. I want to use the honey for the side dish, too."

"Good," said Chef Nancy. "Just remember, you have a delicate fish. You don't want to overpower it."

Rae waved her pantry list when she saw Chef Nancy approaching, and then she whispered, "I can't believe Oliver changed with me. I'm so happy I got mushrooms."

Chef Nancy examined the list. "If everyone is happy, then you'll all do your best." She had a feeling about Oliver and mushrooms. He must not like them. Why else would you give up such a delicious ingredient?

Chef Nancy approached Oliver cautiously. He was pacing back and forth. "So, Oliver, is everything okay?"

He nodded. "Just thinking. Sometimes it helps if I keep moving."

"Any ideas for your recipe?" asked Chef Nancy.

"Something cheesy and spicy."

Chef Gary clapped his hands. "Attention, everyone! We're going to do things a little differently. When I call 'time,' we'll do the pantry run and then move right into cooking without a break."

Caroline looked over at Chef Nancy. They were on their own. No more help.

CHAPTER 29

ROLLING."

Chef Gary raised his hand. "You have five minutes in the pantry. GO!"

Rae grabbed breadcrumbs, Parmesan cheese, lemons, cauliflower, cream cheese, and garlic. She stopped and checked the list inside her basket. She couldn't forget anything—not this time.

Caroline was done before the time limit, but she tried to look busy for the cameras. She took extra time pretending to look for white balsamic vinegar.

"TIME!" called Chef Gary.

Everyone ran back to their workstations.

Chef Gary raised his hand again. "LET'S GET COOKING!"

Oliver, Caroline, and Rae pulled out their fish. They were all starting the same: fillet the fish. Oliver was done first, but Caroline wasn't far behind. Rae took her time—the last thing she wanted was for the judges to have a mouth full of bones.

Chef Aimee and Chef Porter wandered back and forth between the workstations, checking on everyone's progress. Rae wasn't excited to see Chef Porter coming her way, but she forced a smile. "Hello, Chef Porter."

"Hello, Rae. What are you working on?"

Rae dropped the last cauliflower floret into the boiling water. "I'm making roasted garlic cauliflower mash. Next, I'll roast the garlic in the oven."

"I look forward to that," said Chef Porter. "I am something of a fan of roasted garlic."

Rae sliced the top of the garlic and rubbed it with olive oil. "Me too!"

....

Chef Aimee's first visit was with Oliver.

He held out his bowl for her to see. "This will be the crust for the fish. I'm mixing Parmesan cheese, paprika, black pepper, white pepper, thyme, celery seed, cayenne pepper, garlic powder, salt, and breadcrumbs. I'll coat the fish in flour, buttermilk, and then this."

"Frying or baking?" asked Chef Aimee.

"Baking," answered Oliver

"Looks tasty," said Chef Aimee. "I'm glad I'll get to try it."

Oliver added grits to his pot of boiling water, whisked them together, and lowered the heat.

....

Chef Porter and Chef Nancy both arrived at Caroline's workstation at the exact same time. Caroline stopped working and looked up, worried.

"Please continue," said Chef Aimee. "We don't want to interrupt."

"What's that?" asked Chef Porter, interrupting.

Caroline stopped and turned to see what she was asking about. "Radishes. I'm going to roast them with honey."

"Oh! I've never had those before." Chef Nancy smiled. "Can't wait to try them." She coaxed Chef Porter away. "Let's go see over here."

....

"THIRTY MINUTES!"

Oliver rolled his fish fillets in the breading and put them on a greased baking sheet in the oven. The tilapia needed to cook for only fifteen minutes, so there'd be plenty of time for plating. Plating? Oliver looked around frantically. He'd forgotten all about plating. He hadn't picked up anything from the pantry. Nothing green, not even a stalk of parsley. He banged his fist on the table. How could he have been so *stupid!*

Caroline checked the oven. Her trout was cooking perfectly. She'd added a few extra cloves of garlic. She'd heard something about Chef Porter liking them. She smiled and whispered to herself, "Never disappoint a judge."

Rae added morel mushrooms to the garlic in her pan and stirred until they were tender. She peered into the saucepan

on the stove. Her broth of water, rice wine vinegar, soy sauce, Szechwan pepper, and shallots smelled heavenly. She lowered the heat. The flavors had fused—it only needed to stay warm.

"FIFTEEN MINUTES!"

Rae put a skillet on the stove, and while it warmed, she patted her fish dry and sprinkled it with salt and pepper. Once the skillet was hot, she added the fish. A hot pan guaranteed a nice crust. She watched her fish carefully. Delicate fillets cooked in no time.

Caroline added the radish leaves to her skillet of roasted radishes. The leaves wilted and she turned off the heat.

Oliver grumbled and stirred cheddar cheese into his grits. Bland-looking fish, plus bland-looking grits—his plate was going to be a disaster. He needed some color and he didn't have anything.

"FIVE MINUTES!"

····

Rae picked a shallow bowl and placed it on a plate. She put the black cod in the center of the bowl and surrounded it with spicy Szechwan sauce and morel mushrooms. She added dollops of roasted garlic cauliflower mash sprinkled around the edge of the plate, adding cut chives for color.

Caroline put her trout on one side of a rectangular plate, on the other she arranged the radishes and their green leaves into a decorative arrangement. Between the two spaces she placed three drops of spiced honey.

Oliver did the best he could. He put his fillet on the plate opposite three dollops of cooked grits. It wasn't as bad as he thought it would be. The golden fillet stood out on the white plate.

"TIME!"

Six hands went up.

Caroline and Rae were smiling.

There was a five-minute break while Janet and Mark shot video close-ups of the food.

CAROLINE

I feel really good about my fish. I cut a nice fillet and it's well spiced. I think the judges will be surprised by my roasted honey radishes. I tried one and they are delicious. I think Chef Porter will enjoy the spiced honey—sweet and spicy go well together.

Everything worked out just the way I wanted. My spicy Szechwan sauce isn't going to burn anyone's tongue, but it does have flavor. I think it's unexpected with the morels. The cauliflower turned out great too. I used the food processor to mix in the cream cheese, garlic, Parmesan, and chicken broth. It came out so creamy and smooth—not at all like cauliflower.

RAE

OLIVER

My plate is austere. I want the judges to focus on the food, not on decoration. I don't need any visual tricks. My food speaks for itself.

CHAPTER 30

Chef Gary called Oliver, Rae, and Caroline to the front with their plates. "Since this has been a week of family traditions, we thought it would be nice to end together, our cooking family. Caroline, can you tell us what you've made."

Caroline

Caroline straightened up. "I made a honey glazed trout fillet with roasted honey radishes and spiced honey drizzle.

"Yum!" said Chef Aimee.

Chef Gary handed out the forks.

"I like the presentation," said Chef Porter. "It's very colorful, and I can't wait to try those radishes." She speared a radish and took a bite. "Delicious! I am not disappointed."

"The fish is nice," said Chef Gary. "Flaky, moist, and not too sweet."

Chef Aimee waved her hand in front of her mouth. Chef

Gary quickly handed her a glass of water. She guzzled it down, then fanned her mouth. "That spicy honey drizzle is spicy! Too spicy for me!" She took another drink of water.

"I like spice," said Chef Porter. She took a piece of fish. "This is good too." She turned to Caroline. "Well done."

Chef Aimee was still drinking water, so Chef Gary moved on to Rae. "Rae, can you tell us what you made?"

"Yes, Chef. I made Szechwan black cod with a morel mushroom broth. My side dish is roasted garlic cauliflower mash."

"Great presentation!" said Chef Gary. "You sure know how to decorate a plate."

Rae blushed.

Chef Gary took a piece of the cod. "Moist and flavorful." He popped a morel into his mouth and closed his eyes. "Nutty, meaty—with this little spice in the sauce." He nodded. "It works—in fact it's delicious."

Chef Porter scooped up a forkful of the cauliflower. "I can't believe this is cauliflower. I think I like this even better than mashed potatoes."

"Impossible," said Chef Aimee. She picked up her fork and took a bite, then raised her hand. "I could be wrong."

Chef Aimee and Chef Porter both complimented the fish, as well.

Rae couldn't stop smiling.

Oliver was next, and he was not smiling.

Oliver

"Oliver, can you tell us what you've made?"

"I made Cajun-spiced Parmesan crusted tilapia, with smoky cheese corn grits."

"What kind of cheese did you use?" asked Chef Gary.

"Smoked cheddar."

Chef Gary nodded, then shook his head. "This plate looks a little bare for me. I think some color would have been nice. Is this on purpose?"

"Yes, sir, of course. I wanted to keep the plate minimal to focus on the food."

Chef Gary nodded. "Fine, but, looking at it now, if you could add one more ingredient, what would you choose?"

"Roasted mini heirloom tomatoes," answered Oliver.

"Ooh," said Chef Aimee. "That would've been nice." She took a fork and cut off a bite of fish. "It's tender and flakey . . . and not too spicy. Well done, Oliver."

"These grits are to die for," said Chef Gary. "I like them better than the fish. There's a disconnect for me with the crust. Cajun spice and Parmesan cheese. I'm not sure that's working."

Chef Porter agreed. "I think one or the other would have been a better choice." She took another bite of the grits. "But the grits are delicious. Very tasty."

Chef Gary took another mouthful of grits and swallowed fast. "Thank you, Oliver. Good work!"

The judges moved to the back of the room to discuss the

week's competition. Caroline, Rae, and Oliver stood waiting for the final decision.

The decision for the elimination challenge always took the longest. The judges had to evaluate everything: big challenges, mini-challenges . . . everything from the whole week counted.

Finally, they came back. Chef Gary moved to the center of the room. "These young chefs are amazing. They only just learned how to fillet a fish, and not one of us found a bone. They mastered the skill in record time. I wish we could keep you all here for another week, but unfortunately we can't. Someone has to go home. There were some mistakes made today, but they were minor, and that's why today's decision was so difficult.

"Oliver, the crust on your tilapia was a miss, but your smoky cheese grits were outstanding.

"Caroline, your honey trout and your roasted radishes were creative and inventive, but your spicy honey drizzle was a tad too spicy.

"Rae, your black cod and morel sauce was sophisticated and delicious, and we could not get enough of your cauliflower mash. It was unanimous: Rae, you are the winner of this elimination challenge! Congratulations! You will be advancing to next week's competition. Please come and stand at the front."

"YES!" Rae threw her arms into the air and raced around the table to stand next to next to Chef Gary.

Chef Aimee handed her an envelope. "Congratulations! This is a certificate for one thousand dollars' worth of new

cooking supplies. Pretty handy if you win the food truck next week." Rae jumped and screamed! She couldn't believe it. The audience clapped and cheered. Suddenly she remembered Caroline. She looked across the table. Caroline stood motionless.

Chef Porter raised one hand and the room went quiet. "This is unfortunate, but we have to send one of our young chefs home. I have no doubt that we will see this young person again, and in their very own restaurant. Caroline, will you step forward?"

Caroline shakily put one foot in front of the other.

"Caroline," said Chef Aimee. "You may join Rae up at the front."

The room fell into a shocked silence.

Chef Gary shook his head. "Oliver, I am sorry, but you

will not be joining us for week three. While you did accumulate the most stars and win the Golden Envelope for the advantage in the elimination round, many of your wins were for the mini-challenges, things such as fixing the roux, the mushroom challenge, and the fish challenge. Your only substantial win this week was the ratatouille lasagna." Chef Gary paused. "And there was another matter brought to my attention—your burnt dulce de leche. Oliver, please hang up your apron."

Caroline gasped and covered her mouth.

Oliver nodded and looked down.

"Oliver, we were happy to have you here, and I know Chef Porter speaks the truth. There are great things in store for you. Thank you for being part of our show."

Oliver nodded, forced a smile, thanked the chefs, thanked Caroline and Rae, hung up his apron, and then walked up the ramp and out the door. Caroline grabbed Rae's hand and squeezed.

OLIVER

Well, I admit that I'm a little surprised about losing, but I gave it my best shot. I'm still cool, calm, and creative. I made some mistakes, but I'll only become a better chef because of them. I was glad for the experience and happy for Caroline and Rae. Next up—start my own restaurant! I have connections.

Chef Aimee put her arm around Rae's shoulder. "Next week is going to be unbelievable! For both of you." She smiled at Caroline. "Just you wait and see."

I can't believe I won! I can't believe Caroline is here! I can't believe we get one more week together. I don't want to think about having to battle Caroline. We've become like best friends, but tomorrow I'll say, *Yeah, I can win!*

RAE

CAROLINE

Unbelievable! I didn't know that Oliver had burnt his dulce de leche! Unbelievable! I'm so glad I'm here . . . with Rae. It's the best and we're besties! I can't believe it—one of us is going to win the food truck. AAAAAH!

"Congratulations, Caroline and Rae. You are moving on to the last round of *Next Best Junior Chef*! This round of competition will be unparalleled—it's friend against friend. There's no room for helping hands, and one mistake could send you home. Can the besties fly solo? Are they brave enough to face the mystery challenge? Who will be the Next Best Junior Chef? Tune in to the final episode of *Next Best Junior Chef* to find out!"

STAY TUNED FOR SCENES FROM THE SEASON-ONE FINALE OF NEXT BEST JUNIOR CHEF!

But first, a word from our experts . . .

Essential Techniques for the Young Chef

from *The Young Chef: Recipes and Techniques for Kids Who Love to Cook* by the Culinary Institute of America

. . . .

These techniques are the cornerstone of every chef's success. The better practiced you are at these methods, the better a chef you will become—and the better your food will look and taste.

Mise En Place and Measuring

Mise en Place

Mise en place (pronounced "meez en plas") is a French term that means "everything in its place." In the kitchen, it is a

concept that helps chefs become more organized and work more efficiently. Having good *mise en place* means that you have cut, chopped, and measured all the ingredients needed for a recipe before you begin to cook or bake. When you have all your ingredients in front of you, the next step is to review them against the recipe to make sure nothing has been left out and that everything is measured correctly. This organizational concept will allow you to build professional-level work habits that will last forever.

Measuring

Accurate measuring is extremely important to the success of all recipes. Oftentimes just a little bit too much or too little of something can ruin the dish.

There are two types of measuring cups. Dry ingredients use a cup that has a flush rim and that measures exactly the amount stated on the handle. Typically these come in sets containing a ⅛ cup, a ¼ cup, a ⅓ cup, a ½ cup, and a 1 cup. Liquid or fluid measuring cups are clear and have the measurements marked on the side of the container.

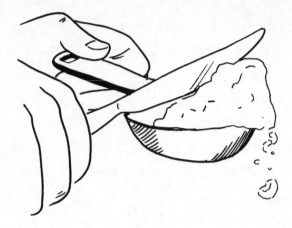

When measuring dry ingredients, scoop—do not pack—the ingredient into the cup, and then level it off with the back of a knife.

When measuring liquid ingredients, place the cup on a level surface, fill it to the desired amount, and then bend down and look closely at eye level to make sure the ingredient is level with the line on the cup.

AND NOW A SNEAK PEEK AT EPISODE 3 OF *NEXT BEST JUNIOR CHEF!*

NEXT BEST JUNIOR CHEF

EPISODE 3

THE Winner IS...

mix it up!

?

by Charise Mericle Harper

CHAPTER 1

Caroline turned away from the studio door and studied Rae's face. "Friends . . ."

". . . to the end!" They finished the sentence together. After two tough weeks of slicing and dicing, they were here together for the final week of competition.

"Shhhhh." Chef Nancy put a finger to her lips.

They nodded and quickly faced forward. In just a few seconds the door would open and it would begin all over again.

Rae counted the days on her fingers and then rubbed her palms against her shirt. In seven days one of them would be the winner—the Next Best Junior Chef! And the other . . . She didn't want to think about that. She studied the back of Caroline's head. Was she nervous about winning or—worse— losing? The producer's voice interrupted her thoughts.

"BOOMS!"

"LIGHTS!"

"CAMERAS!"

"ROLLING!"

And then the announcer began. "Welcome to *Next Best Junior Chef*! This is week three, our FINAL week of competition. After Thursday's elimination round, we'll have a winner for the Next Best Junior Chef! We have two remaining talented junior chefs, who have certainly earned the right to be here, but are they ready for what lies ahead? This week's challenges will test their culinary knowledge, ingenuity, and maybe even the bonds of their friendship. It's time to jump from the frying pan into the fire. Will they sizzle or fizzle? We can't wait to find out—so without further delay, let's bring out our final contestants."

Chef Nancy tapped Caroline's shoulder. Caroline walked confidently to the front of the studio, pacing herself to match the announcer's tempo.

"Congratulations, Caroline, and welcome to this exciting final week of competition. Caroline is eleven years old and from Chicago, Illinois. She worked some fast food magic last week, elevating a hot dog to an *haute* dog. She has continually impressed the judges with her creativity and culinary talent."

Chef Nancy held the door for Rae.

"Congratulations, Rae, and welcome to the final week of competition."

Rae blinked twice, focused on the front, and started down the ramp. The energy of the room quickly changed her nervousness into excitement.

"Rae is eleven years old and from Port Chester, New York. Last week, she won unanimous praise for perfecting a cookie classic and served up a winning dish in the elimination round. This young chef is a master of both pleasing the palate and presentation."

Rae stood next to Caroline in front of the three judges.

"Our esteemed judges include Chef Vera Porter of the famous Porter Farm Restaurant, the renowned pastry chef Aimee Copley, and Chef Gary Lee, restaurant proprietor and host of the award-winning show *Adventures in Cooking*. The judges will be watching our competitors throughout the week, and everything that happens along the way will be taken into consideration when we get to the final elimination round. In addition to choosing a winner, the judges will have to dismiss one of our junior chefs and ask them to hang up their apron. This decision will be based on performance, the taste and presentation of their dishes, and their overall creative vision."

Caroline reached for Rae's hand, then gave it a squeeze and held on. Caroline squeezed back.

"Our junior chefs are mentored by Chef Nancy Patel, the 2013 recipient of the Golden Spoon Award. The winner of *Next Best Junior Chef* will receive two life-changing prizes: a custom food truck *and* a guest spot on *Adventures in Cooking* when it begins filming this summer in Italy!"

Chef Gary stepped to the center of the room. "WOW! This is it!" He nodded to each of the junior chefs. "Congratulations. You've made it!"

They smiled back.

He shook his head. "I have to be honest, this is not going to be an easy week, but"—he raised a finger—"it will be exciting. We have twists, turns, and *lots* of surprises. You will not be disappointed. As in previous weeks, there is a theme, and we're especially excited about this one. Our theme for the week is innovation. So we'll want to see some fresh new ideas. Are you ready to battle it out and flex your creative muscles?"

"YES, CHEF!"

"And you're still friends?" He pointed to their joined hands. "Remarkable! Well, that calls for a celebration. Let's have a toast!" He motioned to an assistant standing at the side of the studio. "Bring out the champagne!"